girls who code

The
Friendship
Code

Hi, I'm Reshma, and I'm the founder of Girls Who Code.

Do you know what coding is? It's essentially telling a computer (or an iPhone or a robot!) what to do. But did you know that it's also about creating, imagining, and inventing awesome things based on anything you're interested in, and above all, having fun with your friends?

Girls Who Code teaches girls in middle school and beyond to write code. We help girls get inspired by all the things they can do when they learn to code—from creating a game that raises awareness about global warming to making a lighting system that can sense the beat in music and create light displays to match. When you learn to code, the possibilities are endless.

When I first started Girls Who Code, I realized that there was a need for books that described what it's like to actually *be* a girl who codes. I always say, "You can't be what you can't see." And that's true for books, too! We need to read stories about girls who look like us in order to be inspired to try something new.

In this book, you'll read about a girl named Lucy and her group of friends who embark on an adventure to learn to code. Lucy and her friends are just like the girls in our programs—they want to build cool things, meet other amazing coders, and have fun!

My hope is that you'll read this book and get inspired to join our movement of tens of thousands of girls across the country—and the globe—who are changing the world through code.

Happy reading—and coding!

Reshma Saujani

Reshma Saujani

PENGUIN WORKSHOP
An Imprint of Penguin Random House LLC, New York

Text and cover illustrations copyright © 2017 by Penguin Random House LLC and Girls Who Code Inc. All rights reserved. Published by Penguin Workshop, an imprint of Penguin Random House LLC, New York. PENGUIN and PENGUIN WORKSHOP are trademarks of Penguin Books Ltd, and the W colophon is a registered trademark of Penguin Random House LLC. Printed in the USA.

Visit us online at www.penguinrandomhouse.com.

Emoji provided free by EmojiOne.

Library of Congress Control Number: 2017953994

ISBN 9780399542510

10 9 8 7

by Stacia Deutsch

Penguin Workshop

Chapter One

"Lucy ... Lucy ... Lucy ..."

"What? Huh?" I was so excited for the bell to ring that I didn't hear my teacher calling my name. "Oh." I raised my head, glanced at the long, sprawling math problem written across the whiteboard, and said, "Four."

Mrs. Clark stared at me for a moment, then looked over her shoulder at the numbers she'd written. "Correct ..." She grabbed an eraser. "That's all for today, class. No homework, so use your time to review today's lesson." The bell rang. "Have a good after—"

I missed the "—noon" because by the time she finished, I was already down the hall.

I'd been waiting for this moment since the day I saw the posting on the Halverston Middle School website, and now here it was. I was *finally* in sixth grade. I was *finally* going to my very first coding club meeting!

I waved hello to my best friend, Anjali, as I passed her in the hall. She was rushing to film club in the opposite direction. "Text me," she called out, though she didn't have to say it. I would have texted, anyway.

I tightened my backpack straps and took off running. I'd already picked out my seat in the computer lab. I wanted to be front and center. I was going to get started right away on an app that would help my uncle and change the world—

Oof!

"Watch where you're going," Sophia Torres scoffed, blocking the way into the computer lab. Tall and fit, she filled the doorway when she spread her arms across it. There wasn't room for me to squeeze past.

"Sorry," I said, looking down at her brand-new tennis shoes. I didn't want to start a fight. I just wanted her to move.

"Geek," Sophia muttered under her breath.

It stung a bit, but I didn't care. It wasn't the first time someone had called me that, and I wasn't going to let anyone ruin coding club for me. There were a few kids at school who intimidated me, but Sophia wasn't one of them. I puffed out my chest. "Shouldn't you be doing sportsy stuff or something?" I was pretty sure Sophia was managing the boys' football team this fall. But we'd barely spoken in months, so I wasn't positive.

She rolled her eyes at me. They were as dark as her hair. "I'm taking Mondays off for this."

I heard footsteps behind me. If I didn't move past Sophia immediately, other kids wouldn't be able to get into the room, either.

I dodged left to pass her, but she blocked my path and laughed.

"Come on, Soph," I said softly, calling her the nickname she'd had since preschool. "You know how important this is to me."

"It's important to me, too," she answered. And with that, Sophia turned and hustled into the room, throwing herself into the seat I wanted. She planted her hands in front of the computer that I'd had mental dibs on.

Sighing heavily, I took the seat at the end of the row and tried to ignore Sophia as the classroom filled with students. Even though we were ex-friends, there was no reason we couldn't be in coding club together. At least that's what I told myself.

A bunch of other kids came into the room before

Mrs. Clark arrived. She tipped her head at me. "Well done, Lucy. You made it here in record time."

I smiled. Mrs. Clark was my favorite teacher, and I was glad she was in charge of the club. She was born in Lebanon, went to England for college, and then came to the United States. She had such interesting stories about traveling the world and the things she did before she decided to become a teacher. Her stories almost made me want to be a teacher like her . . . but only almost. I was going to be a computer programmer, just like my mom. Anjali always joked that my first word wasn't "Dada," but rather "data." She was probably right.

"Alicia Lee . . . Bradley Steinberg . . . Maddie Lewis . . . Mark Lewis . . . ," Mrs. Clark read off the club list. When she hit the name Maya Chung, I whipped my head around. I hadn't seen Maya come in, and wondered what she was doing here. Maya was a seventh-grader and, unlike Sophia, she *was* one of those kids who scared me. Not because she was mean, but because she was really, really cool. She was the president of the student council and wrote a fashion column for the school newspaper. I'd never talked to her, or even made eye contact before, because honestly, what would I say?

I glanced down at my *Doctor Who* T-shirt. Maya would never wear a T-shirt and jeans, at least not without accessorizing with a scarf in her short black hair, or something bold, like a big necklace or earrings. That's what her last column said. I always read it.

Looking at me, no one would guess I was interested in fashion. It's not like I spent a lot of time getting ready in the morning, but I liked reading what Maya wrote and doing some of the things she suggested, like painting my nails light pink. I loved the way they shimmered.

"I'm here," Maya announced with a groan, as if this was the last place on earth she wanted to be. I figured if she wanted to learn coding, she could have started last year— it was offered to sixth-graders and up. I wondered why she was starting now.

Feeling self-conscious, I smoothed down a wrinkle in my T-shirt. Mrs. Clark was still reading names. "Grace Rahman ... Sammy Cooper ... Ellie Foster ... Leila Devi ..."

When were we going to start coding? We were ten minutes into the club time, and Mrs. Clark was still on roll call.

When she seemed like she was almost finished, something *finally* happened.

Beep! Beep! Beep!

But this was not the something I was hoping for. I looked around for a minute before realizing that the noise was coming from my backpack. And it wasn't a soft, buzzy type of beep that could blend into classroom noises, or an echoing kind of beep that I could pretend was coming from the hall. It was a loud, annoying blast that made everyone in the club look in my direction.

"Lucy," Mrs. Clark said with a stern expression. "You know the rules about phones at school. The same applies to after-school programs." She pointed at my bag. "Turn it off and turn it over. I'll keep it for the rest of the club."

My heart was racing, and my face felt like it was on fire. I reached into my bag to find the phone, sure I was having a heart attack. My phone had been on silent all day, like the school rules said, so I had no idea what was going on.

After what seemed like an eternity, I found my phone, flipped it around, and desperately tried to silence it. But the screen stayed dark, and the beeps got louder.

"Put it on vibrate," Maya said, with an exasperated look. It was horrifying that this was the first thing she'd ever said to me.

"I tried, but it's not working," I answered, feeling my face redden even more.

"Try turning it off," Bradley said. He chuckled, his red freckles seeming to twinkle. He clearly thought this was hysterical.

I glared at him. "The screen won't even turn on."

"Try slamming it on your desk," Bradley suggested, snickering to his friends.

I ignored him.

The beeping continued to echo through the classroom as kids shared their ideas. It felt like everyone was shouting at me, which only made my heart beat faster.

Mrs. Clark came over to my desk. With her usual calm, she tucked her long dark hair behind her ears, pushed up her glasses, and held out her hand. I handed her my phone.

For some reason, it finally opened to my main screen. She started swiping around, and I could tell she was looking through my apps.

Suddenly, the beeps stopped. I took a deep breath, and my heartbeat settled.

Mrs. Clark gave me a meaningful glance. "Looks like someone who knows a thing or two about coding made a fake game and downloaded it onto your phone. It's programmed to beep and freeze your phone."

"I . . ."

How was that possible? I hadn't even noticed!

I began to say I had no idea who would do that. It would have to be someone who had access to my phone. And someone who liked to play tricks on me.

"Oh." I knew exactly who had messed with my phone, and from the look on Mrs. Clark's face, she did, too. Two afternoons a week, he was her student.

Mrs. Clark gave me a sympathetic smile. "Say hi to Alex for me when you see him."

"I will," I said, but we both knew that when I got home I was going to have a lot more than "hi" to say to my brother!

Chapter Two

"*I*s Erin Roberts here?" Mrs. Clark asked, scanning the room as if someone might have slipped by her during the phone fiasco. I knew all the other kids, either from my classes or from around school. Mostly we were sixth-graders. Maya and Grace were the only seventh-graders.

"Hmm. Doesn't look like it," she said, setting the roll-call sheet aside. "Okay, then. Let's get started."

Finally!

The computer lab rules said students couldn't turn on the computers until the teacher gave permission. I raised my pointer finger and hovered it over the power button. I was waiting for Mrs. Clark to tell us to "boot up." I could tell some other kids were doing the same thing.

Instead, what we heard was: "I've set out some tables in the back. Gather around."

Mrs. Clark hefted three big brown paper bags into her arms. They'd been tucked in a corner where I hadn't noticed them. "This way." She walked toward the back of the room.

Wait. What? My finger twitched. I must have misunderstood.

I swiveled my chair toward Mrs. Clark and raised my hand.

"Come along, Lucy," she said as most kids got up and went to the tables she'd arranged at the back of the room.

I stayed at the computer station and raised my hand higher, this time waving it.

"Lucy," Mrs. Clark said. "You can't have a question already..."

"But—" I did. I had a thousand questions, the first one being, "Am I in the right place?" Maybe coding club met somewhere else, because I'd expected to be sitting at computers, not at empty tables in the back of the room. How was I going to be the first black girl to win a Turing Award—it's like a Nobel Prize for coding—for my coding skills if we didn't actually use the computers?

I opened my mouth to say all that, but Mrs. Clark cut me off. "Hang on to your question, okay?" She looked at me over her glasses. "There will be time at the end of our club time to answer everything."

"But...I...We...App..." My pointer finger felt heavy, as if it had a brick attached. I pulled it from the power button and walked slowly to the back of the room. Some of the other kids who'd stayed at their computers shuffled along with me—it wasn't like we had a choice.

Mrs. Clark broke us into groups, setting a brown bag in front of each cluster. "Sophia, Maya, and Lucy—you'll be partners. You can take the middle table."

Ugh. Now I was being grouped with people who didn't even care about coding (well, Sophia said it was important to her, but I didn't believe her). I thought maybe this was a cruel joke. Or a dream. In a few minutes, I was going to wake up and discover that I'd fallen asleep in math and that coding club hadn't started yet.

Unfortunately, I was wide awake.

First no computer, then no coding, and now my group was made up of one girl who was my mortal enemy and one who intimidated me ... what more could happen?

The computer lab door opened.

The principal walked in, followed by a girl I didn't recognize.

"You must be Erin," Mrs. Clark said warmly. "You're joining the seventh grade today, right?"

The girl nodded, her blond hair falling over her glasses. When I looked a little closer, it seemed as though she might have been crying. She didn't say anything.

"Welcome to coding club." Mrs. Clark led her over to my table. "We're just getting started. You can join this group." We had three people while the others all had four. Now we were even.

Just because I was mad that we weren't coding yet didn't mean I couldn't be polite. I imagined it would be hard to start at a new school after classes had already begun. Plus, Erin looked like she needed someone friendly, and I didn't trust the others at my table to be that person.

"Hi," I said.

Erin smiled faintly at me and then looked away toward the door. I think if Principal Stephens hadn't closed it when he left, she might have made a run for the hallway.

"All right." Mrs. Clark rubbed her hands together just like she did in math class when she was excited about introducing something new. "Don't touch the bags.

That's for later. We're going to start today's session with a writing assignment." She handed out pencils and index cards. "On your own, without help from your group, write down instructions for how to make a peanut butter and jelly sandwich."

She pulled out a stopwatch. "You have two minutes." She set the timer. "Go."

Um, what? A peanut butter and jelly sandwich? What did this have to do with coding? I raised my hand.

Mrs. Clark gave me a look that unmistakably meant, "Later, Lucy." So I dropped it, figuring the faster we did her activity, the faster we'd get back to the computers.

I grabbed the card and scribbled:

Take two pieces of bread. Open the peanut butter. Spread it on one side of the bread. Open the jelly and spread it on the other side. Put the halves together. Ta-da, peanut butter and jelly sandwich.

I was done in about three seconds. I sat back from the table and watched the others in my group. Maya was drawing a picture to accompany her instructions. She was a really good artist. Sometimes she did drawings to go with her articles in the paper. I wanted to say something to her, but what? She probably didn't even notice I was in her group.

Sophia had written "Rules" on the top of her card and was writing a novel-length book in very small letters about the sandwich. I thought she'd never finish . . . and then she asked for another card.

Erin was sitting back in her chair, like me. But unlike me, she hadn't filled out her card. Instead, she contemplated the ground while biting a fingernail.

I turned away so she wouldn't think I was staring at her.

Other than the scratch of pencils on paper, the only sound in the room was the ticking of the clock. After what seemed like a million ticks, Mrs. Clark collected our index cards.

She shuffled them, saying, "I'm going to make a sandwich. I just don't know how . . ." And after an overly dramatic pause, she added, "Oh, look, I'll use Lucy's instructions." She held up my card, putting the rest aside. "Bradley, come help me."

Bradley was a joker, but he was also the second best student in my math class. As he went to stand by Mrs. Clark, I wished we were in the same group. He was with Maddie and Mark, really funny twins. That group was bound to be more exciting than mine. Plus, with Bradley being so good at math . . . I bet he could help me with my app.

Mrs. Clark handed him my instructions. "Read them step by step," she said.

"'Take two pieces of bread.'" He over-emphasized the words.

She raised one of the paper bags and pulled out a brand-new loaf of bread. She stared at the loaf, turning it around in her hands.

I wanted to hurry this along. It was a waste of precious coding time.

"Two pieces . . ." Mrs. Clark tore the plastic bread bag down the middle and picked out one slice of bread and a bit of crust from a second slice. "A crust is a 'piece of bread.' Isn't it?" she asked Bradley.

I blurted out, "I meant that you should undo the twist tie to open the bag and take the first two slices. No one likes the crusts."

Mrs. Clark stared at me as if I was speaking an alien language. She turned back to Bradley. "What's next?"

"'Open the peanut butter.'"

She took a jar out of the paper bag and set it on the

table. "We are using sunflower butter," she explained. "In case anyone has allergies. But we'll pretend it's peanut." She turned to Bradley. "How should I open it?"

He gave her a blank look.

"You mean Lucy's instructions don't say?" she said.

Bradley got a twinkle in his eye. "You could slam it on the desk!" Kids chuckled.

"Other ideas?" Mrs. Clark asked.

Taking their cue from Bradley, kids started spouting out crazy ideas. Sammy suggested dropping the jar from the school roof. Maddie and Mark came up with a plan that involved pliers and a hammer. Another girl at Sammy's table, Leila, had an idea that involved ropes and pulleys and a sharp battle-ax. Mrs. Clark had to cut her off because she was taking forever to describe it.

I heard a small chuckle next to me and saw that Erin had raised her head. Now she was interested.

"No. No. No," I said when I couldn't take it anymore. "What I meant was to use your wrist to open the jar."

Mrs. Clark hit the lid with her wrist and frowned. "It didn't work."

"You have to wrap your fingers around the lid and turn it," Sammy said.

She wrapped her fingers loosely but didn't clasp the jar. The lid swiveled around under her palm.

It went on like this for a while, until Sophia said, "Put your hand over the lid, lower it until the jar touches your palm, tighten your fingers, and now rotate the lid counterclockwise while holding the jar still."

Mrs. Clark did exactly what Sophia said, and it worked! I was annoyed that she'd figured out how to get Mrs. Clark to open the jar, but at least we were making progress.

With the jar finally open, Mrs. Clark asked Bradley what was next. "Lucy said, 'Spread it on one side of the bread.'"

"With what?" she asked. When he shrugged, Mrs. Clark stuck her fingers in the jar and scooped out a glob. She spread it along the crust edge.

"I meant . . . ," I started, but I was getting the point. My instructions weren't very good.

In the end, Mrs. Clark handed me a sandwich with one plain piece of bread and a smear of sunflower butter on the bit of crust. I'd only said to spread jelly on the "side," so she'd spread it on the side of the sunflower butter jar. Since I hadn't made it clear which halves went together, she'd rolled the bread and crust together like a burrito. I took the "sandwich" from her sticky fingers, wondering if anyone in the club had thought to mention a knife. Or a napkin.

Now it was our turn. Using what was in the paper bags at each of our tables, we had to make a sandwich following someone else's instructions. Since Erin hadn't filled out her card and mine was already used, Maya and I read Sophia's instructions while Sophia and Erin read Maya's. Turned out, Sophia had done everything the rest of us missed. She mentioned a knife *and* a napkin. *And* she'd suggested putting the sandwich on a plate. Her index-card novel was perfect, and so was the sandwich we made.

When Mrs. Clark asked her what her method was, Sophia explained, "Writing rules for sports isn't so different. You have to think of every way someone might misunderstand and cover for that."

When had Sophia gotten so smart? I felt disappointed and a little angry that she had done better than me. This was supposed to be *my* club. Sophia had her own clubs.

I hoped at least the groups were temporary. Maybe next week I could be with Bradley or Leila.

"Okay, kids, that's all for today," Mrs. Clark said as she wiped the sunflower butter and jelly off her fingers with a napkin. "I want you to think about what today's exercise might mean, and tell me what you came up with at our next club meeting. See you all next Monday."

Whoa. I raised my hand. "This is coding club, not cooking, right?"

Mrs. Clark nodded.

"So when are we going to make an app?"

"Slow down, Lucy," Mrs. Clark told me. "It's not that easy. Plus, you've just taken your first step."

"But I *need* to make an app. How is this," I said, waving my hand at the jars of sunflower butter and jelly, "going to help?"

Apparently I wasn't the only one who thought making sandwiches was not what we had signed up for. Other kids started speaking up.

"Yeah—I want to make an app to track hockey scores."

"And I need an app to find ice-cream trucks!"

"I want to make something that can do my homework for me!"

I chimed in. "My uncle has cancer, and I *have* to make an app to help him."

The room fell silent, and everyone turned toward me.

Mrs. Clark took a long look at me. "Lucy, that is important, but we need some basic skills before we try to help cancer patients—or find ice cream." She had that look she got when she changed her mind about something. She pointed at each of our groups. "Look at your sandwiches."

"Mine is a jar of peanut butter sitting on a folded loaf of bread," Sammy said, looking at the mess on his table.

"You're lucky you got a loaf of bread," Bradley snorted. "I got two jars and no bread. I can't believe I forgot to mention bread!"

Mrs. Clark smiled. "Now you know about input and output. Your instructions are input, and the sandwich is output. What you put into your coding in a computer determines exactly what comes out the other side—just like your instructions for how to make a sandwich." She gathered her things and held the door open for us to leave. "That's it for today."

I smiled at Mrs. Clark. I had a feeling this coding thing was going to be a bit different than what I'd imagined.

Chapter Three

"Mom! Dad! I'm home!" I rushed into the kitchen. My parents were both sitting at the counter, staring at their laptops. Mom was a software programmer and worked from home, though she sometimes had to go to her company's office for meetings. Dad was an artist. He had a studio downtown, but he liked to work on his designs at home. Even though there was office space in the basement, they preferred to work next to each other, upstairs.

The only sound was the clicking of keyboards—they hadn't even heard me come in. "Where's Alex?" I asked, dropping my bag on the floor. There was a third laptop covered with band stickers that sat unopened at the end of the counter.

"Oh, hi, honey!" Mom said, raising her eyes from the screen. "Alex isn't home yet. He had a college counseling appointment."

I grabbed a drink from the fridge. From where I stood behind her, I couldn't see what she was writing. All I could see was her reflection. We looked a lot alike: same dark skin, brown eyes, and thick hair—I liked to wear mine in two long braids, and she preferred hers short.

"Why? And how was coding club?" Mom asked me, focusing on her computer again.

"It was fine," I said, not wanting to get into it. "I just need to talk to Alex, that's all." *And give him an earful about his lousy prank*, I thought.

"He should be back for dinner," Dad said, filling in the shading for the sketch of a sculpture on his touchpad.

Artists have this reputation for being hip and cool, but not my dad. He was way nerdier than Mom. When they met in college, Mom thought his heavy glasses and rumpled clothing were adorable. I'd seen pictures of the two of them back then. If Sophia thought I was a geek, she should have seen my parents. There was no contest.

"We have a dinner guest." Dad tipped his head toward the living room. "Uncle Mickey is here."

"He is?!" There was no one more wonderful than my uncle. He was my dad's twin, and an artist, too. But they made different kinds of art—Dad created modern sculptures, and Uncle Mickey was an abstract painter. He lived about an hour away. Whenever he came to town, Mickey would tell us crazy stories about gallery openings and the celebrities who collected his paintings.

I was about to rush off to see him when Dad warned, "Keep it quiet, Lu. He might be napping."

"Oh," I answered, feeling my spirits drop. I made a point of tiptoeing around the corner, breathing quietly so as not to disturb Uncle Mickey if he was asleep. The back of the couch faced me, so I cautiously peered over it to see if he was lying down. He wasn't there.

"I'm outside," a voice called out.

I hurried to the back porch where Uncle Mickey sat on our old glider, rocking a little. He looked much older and thinner than the last time I'd seen him. "Sit with me." Uncle Mickey patted the seat next to him on the glider.

I walked over and leaned into his open arms for a hug. "I'm glad you're here," I told him, feeling his slight arms wrap around me.

"Good to see you, too, kid. I have a doctor's appointment

in the city tomorrow, so your parents invited me to stay over tonight."

Before getting cancer, Uncle Mickey was the healthiest guy I knew. Unlike my dad, he was always outside when he wasn't in his studio. Even though he was a little pudgy in the middle (exactly like my dad), Mickey could climb mountains.

Now he couldn't climb stairs, and there was no pudge left.

I leaned back on the glider and enjoyed the rocking motion. "Have you painted anything lately?" I asked.

Uncle Mickey sighed. "On my good days. I only have a few more treatments, so I should be back at it soon." He changed the subject. "Tell me about my favorite niece." I was his only niece.

I'd started telling him about school and explaining my disappointment about the coding club when Mom popped her head outside. "You asked me to remind you to take your pills," she said to Uncle Mickey, stepping onto the porch.

"Right, thanks." Uncle Mickey turned to me. "Hang on to that thought, kiddo." He started digging in a tote bag on the ground nearby. He pulled out a large plastic bag filled with prescription bottles and checked a label. "Hmm, not that one, not yet, I don't think," he mumbled, placing it back in the bag. He picked up another bottle and took off the lid.

Mom handed him a small glass of water. He swallowed several greenish-colored pills, then asked Mom to remind him again in a few hours.

"Of course," she said, taking the empty glass and heading back to the kitchen.

"Now," he said to me, "tell me about the coding clu—" He stopped and looked down at his tote bag. "Hang on." There was a bottle of pills in the bottom that he'd missed. "I think I forgot to take the pink one," he said. "These are new. Lucy, would you mind grabbing me more water?"

"Sure," I said. "Be right back."

While I refilled his glass, I was reminded why I wanted to do coding club in the first place. *This was the reason!*

It wasn't the first time Uncle Mickey had come to stay at our house since he was diagnosed with leukemia, a form of cancer. During the past year, I'd often seen him do this exact same thing with his pills. I knew he had one of those plastic pill-organizing boxes with the days of the week marked on it, but he kept having to take new pills, so he didn't always fill the pill organizer. And it's not like a plastic pillbox could remind him to take his pills. Once, he left an important bottle at home and we had to call the doctor and get a few tablets to hold him over for a couple days.

I had an idea for an app that would solve all that. Not just for Uncle Mickey, but for anyone who needed pills, or even just vitamins (which I usually forgot to take). It would remind them which pills to take and when. It would also register when they took the pills and send an alert if they needed refills. I knew there were already some apps like that, even though Uncle Mickey didn't want to use them—he kept saying they wouldn't help. I thought I could create an even better one that I was sure he'd like. It would have cool features like setting up texts and group chats with family members and friends so that they could remind you to take pills, pick them up for you—or even take you to doctors' appointments.

I glanced outside to where Uncle Mickey was waiting. I had to learn coding fast so I could make my app. Days like today were a waste of time.

"Mom," I said. "I need your help."

She grabbed salad from the fridge for dinner. "With what, honey?"

"Coding club is going way too slowly. We didn't even use the computers today."

"Well, it was just the first day, wasn't it?" she said, taking the cutting board out of the cupboard. "Coding takes time to learn."

I looked outside and saw Uncle Mickey nodding off, so I figured I had a few minutes. "I know, but I want to move faster."

"Lu, you know how we feel about shortcuts," Dad said, peering at me over his junky grocery-store reading glasses. "I didn't jump from drawing stick figures to welding big sheets of metal. I had to learn design, engineering, and chemistry before I was ready to do that."

I started rolling my eyes at him, but he gave me a serious look. "Everything worth doing takes time," he added. I'd heard that a thousand times.

"I know, but if Mom could just help me a little . . . ," I explained. "I can still learn most of what I need from Mrs. Clark—I'd just have a little head start."

Mom and Dad exchanged a look. "I could have given you a head start by teaching you some programming years ago, but you were never interested," Mom said. She patted my hand. "I'm so glad you got interested this year, but now that you're in the coding club, we want you to follow the program." She added, "You can always come to me with questions, but I don't want to interfere with Mrs. Clark's curriculum."

"Just like Alex," Dad added. "He's an excellent coder, and he began with Mrs. Clark, like you."

"But we didn't even do any coding today!" I repeated, my voice rising. "And it's a whole week until the next club meeting. What if we don't do any coding again then? It'll take me forever to learn, at this rate." I knew there were coding tutorials online, but I hadn't found anything I could really learn from. They all seemed geared toward people who already knew a bit about coding, or were in a class. That's why I had thought the coding club would be helpful for me.

"That's probably true regardless," Dad said in his always mellow, soft voice, giving Mom a knowing look. "It takes a long time to get proficient in anything."

"But I—"

Slam. The front door closed with a bang.

Alex was home. In a flash, an idea came to me. My brother was eighteen—a senior in high school. Like Dad said, Alex was a really good coder. Maybe, once I explained to him why I needed to learn coding, he'd be willing to help give me a head start. Plus, it would make up for the phone prank he'd pulled on me.

Thing was, Alex never wanted to help me with anything. He had a girlfriend, college applications to fill out, and a job at the pizza parlor. I knew that getting him on board was going to be hard, but it was worth a try.

First, I needed to give Uncle Mickey his water so he could take the pill he almost forgot. "Don't go anywhere," I told Alex as he walked into the kitchen. "I need to talk to you."

Alex looked at me with a big grin on his face and set his bag down. Over the summer, he'd let his hair grow long into curly springs. It was a look I was pretty sure he'd regret. At least he'd shaved off the mini-mustache he'd been unsuccessfully trying to grow over the past few months.

Mom offered to take the water to Uncle Mickey, and Dad went downstairs to put the computers away in the office. He asked me and Alex to set the table for dinner.

"So, how was coding?" Alex asked me, grabbing forks and knives.

I glared back at him. "You've got to stop with the tricks, Alex. Having my phone beep like that was really embarrassing, and it wouldn't stop for the longest time!"

He put his hands up. "What are you talking about? You

can't blame me for your phone problems, Lu."

"C'mon, Alex, I *know* it was you," I told him. "But I am going to forgive you," I said slowly. I wanted to move on. "I'm having some issues in coding club and I need your help."

"Oh yeah? You've got the best teacher."

"I know . . . but the coding stuff is moving too slowly, and I don't have time to wait."

"What's the rush?"

I set plates down on the table and looked up at him. "I want to make an app for Uncle Mickey to help him take his medicine. You know how forgetful he is about his pills." Alex considered this and nodded.

"I tried to get him to download a reminder app, but he didn't like any of the ones I found. I know exactly what kind of app he'd like—one where we, and Mom and Dad, could put in reminders for him. We could use it to remember when he has doctors' appointments, too, so we could help him if he needed it."

Alex seemed interested in my idea, which gave me hope. "Can you help me learn how to code a little faster so I can get started on an app? Give me some tips, maybe?"

"That's a really cool idea, Lu, but you gotta start with the basics. And don't get too ahead of yourself—making an app can take years. Maybe you should focus on a computer program first. Once you have a good foundation, you can do anything."

Ugh, he sounded just like Mom and Dad.

"And then I might even help you." Alex's eyes had a playful glimmer as he set plates down on the table. "Plus, think of all the fun you'll have once you learn how to code!" He made a *beep-beep* sound, with a big smirk on his face.

"You're evil," I said, glaring at him.

"What, me?" he answered, his hands on his chest, trying to look innocent.

I could see that he was not only *not* going to help me, but that I also had to be on guard. He'd played tricks on me my whole life—usually stupid ones like coloring my face when I was sleeping, putting pebbles in my shoes, or hiding all my socks. Sometimes, like today, the tricks were publicly embarrassing. I got the feeling that now that I was in coding club, the pranks were going to move to the next level.

All the more reason why I needed to learn how to code, *ASAP*.

After dinner, I went to my room and searched online

again for how to make an app. There was a kid at school who taught himself to play piano from videos, and he was really good. I figured there was no reason coding couldn't be like that for me.

I found a video that looked promising: Beginner Coding.

But . . . the video was so boring, I dozed off and woke up when it ended.

Instead of trying to watch it again, I clicked on a different video—a variation of the same title. But this one was so fast, I didn't understand anything the woman said after, "So you want to learn to code . . ."

Just when I was about to give up, I got a text. It was Anjali.

A: hey!!! what's up?

L: ugh don't ask 😩 😩 😩

A: what happened??? Is it alex?? 😡 😡 😡 😡

L: sorta but ugh notttt 😣

A: what then?? 🫤 🫤

L: coding. its wayyyy too slow

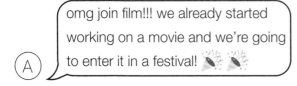

A omg join film!!! we already started working on a movie and we're going to enter it in a festival! 🎬 🎬

That didn't help! How come her club was actually doing stuff?!

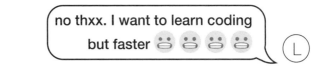

no thxx. I want to learn coding but faster 😬 😬 😬 😬 **L**

I'd already told her about Uncle Mickey and my app idea.

A k . . . maybe I can help??

how? **L**

A idk yet 🤔

💜 💜 💜 💜 **L**

I had no idea how Anjali could help me, but it made me feel better that she would try to. She was one of those people who liked to "fix" things—not like an engineer, more like a person who connected other people and made things happen. Maybe she *could* somehow come up with a solution!

Chapter Four

The next morning, I met Anjali on the stairs outside school. She had long, wavy dark hair that took her forever to style. Today it was in a braid down her back. Unlike me, she wore makeup, usually brightly colored eyeshadow and lip gloss.

"Hey girl," she said, giving me a hug. "Nice earrings." Maya's latest article in the school newspaper had talked about heart studs, so I'd gotten a pair and was giving them a try. I thought they looked cute with my pink shirt and blue jeans.

"Thanks! Cool eyeshadow," I said, admiring the shimmery green hue.

"Trying a new one today," she said, batting her eyes playfully. "Hey, so I was thinking about the coding thing you mentioned last night."

"Oh yeah? Did you come up with an idea for how I'm going to become a coding expert?" I said, jokingly.

"You know me, I've got some ideas up my sleeve."

I laughed. "Of course you do!"

We usually had more time to chat before class, but Anjali was in a rush today. "We have a quiz in social studies, and I want to look over my notes. Let's talk at lunch, okay?"

"'Kay," I said as Anjali rushed off.

I was passing by Mrs. Clark's classroom on my way to class when something caught my eye. Was that Alex in there? Why would he be at the middle school? The high school was in a different building, and there was no reason for him to be here. Unless . . . was he up to no good again?

Classes were going to start soon, but I needed to make sure Alex wasn't making more trouble for me. I peeked in through the doorway of Mrs. Clark's classroom. It was definitely Alex, and he and Mrs. Clark were talking and laughing. I saw him hand her a paper. What was he plotting? I started imagining how he was going to embarrass me again in coding club and clenched my fists.

Suddenly the door swung open. "You're a terrible spy,

Lu," he said. "I knew you were out here the whole time."

"I just got here, and I *wasn't* spying," I said defensively. "But what are you even doing here? You better not be plotting something new, Alex, 'cause if you prank me again in coding—"

"Cool it, Lu. This has nothing to do with you. Mrs. Clark's going to write me a college recommendation." He smoothed a hand over his curls. Mrs. Clark also taught coding at his high school, and he'd been learning coding since he was my age. "I forgot to give her the form when I saw her at school. So I brought it here."

"Really?" I squinted at him. It was hard to believe him sometimes.

"Yes, really." Alex put his hand on my shoulder. "Not everything's about you, Lu."

"Whatever," I said, shaking off his hand. "I've got to get to class."

"Make sure to keep an eye on that phone of yours!" he said, grinning, as I walked away.

Ugh, I *knew* he was up to something!

If the morning at school was weird, after lunch it got even weirder. Anjali never showed up at the cafeteria. I texted her, but she didn't reply. After a while, I figured she got busy and wasn't coming (she often worked on extracurricular stuff during lunch), so I sat with some other friends, including Bradley from coding.

"Boring," he said, wiping cold pasta sauce off his chin with his sleeve. "Snoozefest."

"I actually like this pasta," I said. It was the only school lunch that was halfway decent.

"Not lunch—coding," he clarified. "Making sandwiches is boring. And stupid."

"Yeah," Sammy from coding club added, messily wrapping spaghetti around his fork. "It was pointless."

"Well, we actually did learn something about input and output," I said, not sure why I was defending the activity that had frustrated me, too.

Bradley yawned. "Like I said, B-O-R-I-N-G."

"And a waste of food!" Sammy added.

I went back to eating my pasta. What did I care if they didn't get the point of the activity?

"Want to know what's not boring?" Bradley said. "Making rockets." He looked toward a window and pointed outside, where a group of kids were hanging out with the new science teacher. He was showing them how to launch empty bottles into the air using a bike pump.

"Then why don't you join the science club instead of coding club?" I suggested. He was starting to annoy me.

"Science club would *definitely* be more fun," Bradley answered. "But I want to go to Mars, and you gotta know how to code for that."

"Why do you need to know how to code to go to Mars?" Sammy asked, pasta dotting his chin.

I'd seen a documentary about that on TV. "They use coding to program the computers and machines on the spaceships to do stuff," I explained.

Bradley nodded "Yeah, my dad says code is the foundation for *everything*."

"Well, not everything," I said, but I understood what he meant. Coding was important for the things both Bradley and I wanted to do.

After lunch, I headed to my locker to get books for class.

Taped to my locker was an envelope with my name handwritten on it. Confused, I looked up and down the hall to see who might have left it, but I didn't see anyone other than the usual kids at their own lockers.

Hmm. I checked the envelope again, double-checked

that the name on the front was mine, and after another glance up and down the hall, opened it.

On a white sheet of paper, a typed note read:

```
if (you_want_to_learn_code) {
    do_everything_I_tell_you ( );
}
```

I recognized the parentheses from the first coding video I watched online . . . just before I fell asleep. This definitely looked like programming language.

I read the note again, ignoring the parentheses and strange squiggly things. If I wanted to learn to code, I was going to have to do everything someone said? That sounded like someone wanted to boss me around, and I didn't like that. Was this a joke? Who could the note be from?

"Hey!"

I was so deep in thought, I jumped at the voice.

I turned my head to find Anjali laughing. "Ha—scared ya!" She peeked over my shoulder. "What's that?"

"A note," I told her. "I found it taped to my locker."

"Really? Can I see?"

For some reason, I was reluctant to hand it over. Plus, I was annoyed that she hadn't showed up at the cafeteria earlier.

I turned around, holding the note to my chest. "Where were you at lunch?" I asked.

"Oh yeah, sorry," she said. "I lost track of time. Film club had a meeting. We need an actress who can sing, so we were talking about ideas."

She seemed like she felt bad, so I decided to forget the lunch thing. "Why don't you ask someone who's in theater or choir?"

"We've asked around, but everyone seems busy with their own club's stuff." While she talked, I noticed that Anjali was staring at my note. I had been holding it against my chest but didn't realize the words were facing out.

"'*If you want to learn code, do everything I tell you*'? That's so strange. Who's it from?" Anjali asked, changing the subject.

I turned the note around and looked at it again.

"No idea," I admitted. "Oh, wait a minute," I said, snapping my fingers. "I bet it's from Alex! I saw him talking to Mrs. Clark today. It must be another one of his stupid pranks."

"I bet you're right." Anjali took the note and looked at it carefully, running a finger over the strange punctuation marks. "This is coding language, right?" she said.

I nodded. "Looks like it."

Anjali nodded. "It's got to be from Alex," she said assuredly. "So what are you going to do?"

I thought about it. Alex couldn't win. No way was I going to do "everything" my brother said. That was a recipe for disaster.

I crumpled the note in a ball and shoved it in my locker, slamming the door. "Bye-bye, Alex," I said. "You can't trick me. Not this time!"

Arm in arm, Anjali and I walked off to class together. I'd show my brother who was the boss!

Chapter Five

I didn't go to my locker again until the final bell rang. But I saw the white envelope from down the hall. It was taped to my locker door, just like the first one. I knew before I even got close enough to read the writing that my name was on the front.

Ugh, Alex was at it again. I opened the envelope. The note said:

```
if (you_agree_to_my_terms) {
    grab_a_friend ( );
    go_to_school_playground ( );
}
```

I wondered how long the note had been there. Underneath the first part was another message:

```
if (you_go_to_school_playground) {
    look_under_benches ( );
    find_a_big_yellow_envelope ( );
}
```

And then, after another line break, a third part:

```
if (you_find_the_envelope) {
    trust_me ("You will learn to code");

}
```

"Alex?" I called out, looking down the hall. I only saw kids at their lockers. "Are you here somewhere?" I said, turning the other way.

"Who?" The new girl, the one who cried before coding club, was standing a few feet away. I racked my brain for her name. It finally popped into my head: Erin!

"Oh, hey. Alex is my brother," I explained. "I thought maybe he was lurking around here somewhere."

"What's he look like?" she asked. I described his curly hair.

"I haven't seen anyone like that. But I've only been here a few minutes," she said. She spun the dial of her locker, and the door clanged open. "New locker," she said. "They didn't have one for me yesterday."

"Cool," I replied, not sure what to say.

I turned back to my locker when Anjali came up beside

me. The school buses were leaving soon, and we rode together whenever we could.

Erin started stacking her books on her locker shelf.

Anjali positioned herself between us. "Another note?" she asked me.

I felt a bit guilty, like I should have introduced Erin to Anjali. But I had to talk to Anjali. It was important. I could be extra-friendly to Erin later.

I showed Anjali what I found.

"Maybe you *should* go to the playground," she said. "Just to check it out."

"No way. I'm sure it's from Alex," I told her, putting away my books. "And I don't trust him."

"Maybe he changed his mind and wants to help you," Anjali suggested. I had told her about asking him for help, and how he'd refused.

I snorted. "Not possible."

"Maybe your mom forced him to help you."

"I shook my head. She wants me to learn from coding club."

I stuffed the note in my locker, along with the other one. "I don't want to follow his instructions, anyway. You know how horrible he can be. I think I'll just go home on the bus with you."

"Aren't you even curious?" Anjali reached around me and held my locker door open. She took out the new note and read it aloud.

```
if (you_agree_to_my_terms) {
    grab_a_friend ( );
    go_to_school_playground ( );
}
```

"Where's your sense of adventure?"

I noticed over Anjali's shoulder that Erin was still going through her books at her locker.

I focused back on Anjali. "If he was your brother, you'd know there was no adventure."

"You're being ridiculous." She pushed the note into my hand. "You should go."

"No, I *shouldn't*, Anjali," I said. "The note says I need a friend, and you're busy, right?" She'd mentioned having something to do after school today.

"Yeah, I have an orthodontist appointment," Anjali said.

"I could go with you," a soft voice said from behind Anjali.

Erin had her backpack slung over one shoulder, ready to head out.

"I . . ." She looked from Anjali to me and back. "I didn't mean to eavesdrop, but you two talk kind of loud."

"Truth," Anjali said with a small chuckle. She held out her hand, introduced herself, and then introduced me.

"I know Lucy," Erin said, quickly adding, "sort of."

"Erin's in coding club," I explained.

"Oh, neat!" Anjali said. "Are you liking it?" She gave me a look. "Lucy here thinks it's going way too slow."

"Well, I kind of had no option but to join," Erin said, shrugging her shoulders.

"What do you mean?" I said.

"Long story," she replied. She clearly didn't want to get into it.

"Hey, I have an idea!" Anjali stepped away so that Erin and I were closer together. "Lucy's brother, Alex, is going to help Lucy learn coding to speed things along, and you, Erin, can help her, too! He left these notes in code-speak on Lucy's locker, and now she has to go to the playground to do some mysterious activity."

"You don't have to go," I said to Erin. "Whatever he left there is probably lame, anyway."

"It's okay," Erin said. "I was going to walk home and help my mom unpack." She gave me a small smile. "You'd

46

be saving me from sorting silverware and plates."

"Then it's settled," Anjali said, patting me on the back. "I gotta go."

Erin turned to me as Anjali jetted down the hallway to the buses.

"So," she said, adjusting her backpack strap over her shoulder, "which way's the playground?"

Chapter Six

"'*If (you agree to my terms)* . . .' What do you think this first part means?" Erin asked me, holding my latest locker note as we went outside.

It was a chilly fall day. Erin had put a knit cap over her blond hair and tucked loose strands under it. The school playground was just behind our building, next to the elementary school. There were usually a ton of kids there, especially on a nice day.

"I have to do everything he says, if I want to learn." I showed her the first note, which I'd taken from my locker. I figured it couldn't hurt to have both.

She read it over. "Oh, okay. Well, do you agree?" she asked me. "To do anything the notes say to do?"

She handed me back both notes.

48

"I guess so. I mean, going to the playground means I already sort of did, right?" I sighed, hoping I wasn't making a huge mistake. I didn't want Alex to think I'd do anything he said. I told myself that if he asked me to do anything ridiculous—like clean his gross room or wash his beat-up car—there was no way I'd do it.

"My brother pranks me all the time," I explained to Erin. "Most of his jokes are really annoying. Well, I guess sometimes they're funny, but I never admit it." I gave her a sideways look. "If you ever meet him, you better not tell him I said that."

She laughed and put a hand over her heart. "Your secret's safe with me."

I glanced at the latest note again. *"Look for a big envelope taped under the closest bench,"* I read out loud. What did "closest" mean?

"Closest to the middle school?" I asked Erin.

"Or to the path?" she suggested.

"Or the drinking fountain?" I wondered.

"Or maybe the kid in the red sweatpants," Erin said, half joking. He was on roller skates and struggling to get across the playground by grasping each bench as he passed it.

In the end, we picked the bench closest to the path, which was also closest to the middle school. It was metal and slightly weathered. I looked underneath the solid black seat, and there, just like the note promised, was a large envelope.

Erin clapped her hands, excited about finding it.

"Open it, Lucy," she said in a rush. It was nice to see her enthusiastic about something after she had looked so sad at coding club.

The yellow envelope was bulkier than I'd expected—not that I'd known what we'd find, but still, I was surprised. I tore open the flap and peeked inside. There was a piece of paper and a strip of soft black fabric.

"That's weird," I said, waving the cloth around. It was long and narrow. "Is it a scarf?"

Erin took the fabric and playfully wrapped it around her shoulders, tossing the ends over her back. In a fancy French accent she said, "Ve are ready for ze opera," her green eyes shining.

I chuckled.

Then she took the cloth, wrapped it around her head like a 1980s aerobics sweatband, and said, "Dude, this is totally radical to the max."

She wrapped the scarf around her head several times, covering her eyes, and moaned. "Beware the mummy's curse!"

I laughed so hard, my side hurt. "You should be a comedian! You're so funny!"

"You should hear me sing," she said with a smile.

"Really?" I said. I could totally imagine her onstage. She'd be great.

Erin slowly unwrapped the scarf. She looked at me with a spark in her eyes. "What if it's a blindfold?" she suggested.

"You think?" It could easily be tied as a blindfold, plus it was black. No light would get through.

"Are there instructions?"

I had been so entertained by Erin's antics that I hadn't bothered to look at the paper that was in the envelope. I took it out and read:

> One of you wears the blindfold. The other gives directions through the obstacle course on the map. The blindfolded one shouldn't ask questions, and can't be physically guided by the direction-giver. Be sure to follow the instructions exactly. Good luck.

"What map?" I asked, turning over the paper. The other side was blank.

Erin peeked inside the large envelope. "There's still something in here." She turned it over and shook out a smaller envelope. It had my name on it, and there was a map inside.

"I guess if the map is addressed to me, then you should wear the blindfold," I reasoned. Alex wouldn't have known who was going to come with me to the playground.

Erin held the scarf out in front of her, and this time, instead of acting silly with it, put it over her eyes. "Okay, tie it tight," she told me.

Once the blindfold was on, I looked at the map. "Please don't let Alex embarrass me . . . ," I whispered to myself. Then I glanced at Erin. "Ready?"

I had to send Erin up the steps and down the slide, weave her around the swings, and have her crawl under the monkey bars. The course ended with a trip across the wooden beam that surrounded the sand pit, as if it was a balance beam.

According to the note, Erin couldn't ask me questions and I couldn't physically guide her, so I had to give her detailed directions. "Starting with your right leg, take two steps forward. Stop. Now starting with your left leg, take two to the left side," I told her. I tried to give her measurements, like, "Move one foot's length" after checking the size of her foot in relation to the distance she needed to travel.

Erin followed every word, and when I wasn't perfectly clear, she stopped and waited for better instructions.

By the time she finished the "balance beam" activity and jumped off, I was feeling proud of myself. Erin had gotten through every obstacle perfectly! She tugged down the blindfold, and we high-fived each other.

"That was fun!" I said. I looked down at the notes I was holding. "But what could it have to do with coding?"

"Well, it was kind of like the sandwich exercise in coding club yesterday," she said, folding up the blindfold. "Like, having to give someone really precise instructions for them to do something."

I hadn't thought about it, but the two exercises were actually pretty similar.

Erin patted me on the back. "And you did so much better at giving instructions this time!"

"I guess I did!" I said. "I don't see how this is going to

help me learn how to code faster, though." I was starting to think this was another stupid prank of my brother's, and that he had no intention of helping me learn how to code, after all.

"Looks like it's more of that input/output stuff Mrs. Clark was telling us about," Erin said. "Like, if this was a computer program and you told me to climb onto the third monkey bar instead of the second, we'd have a serious"—she put her hand over her mouth, about to sneeze—"guy-go problem!"

Wait a minute—did she just sneeze, or say "guy-go"? I didn't want to embarrass her, so I didn't mention it.

"Ha-ha—true!" I said. "Well, if it was meant to teach the same thing, at least I did do better than in coding club."

"Totally," Erin answered. She took her phone out of her coat pocket and checked the time. "Ugh, I better go before my mom starts calling me. There are books to put away and towels to fold," she said, rolling her eyes. "I hate moving." She coughed a few times. It was getting a bit chilly.

I'd never moved before, so I wasn't sure what to say. There was one thing I could do, though. "I could help you this weekend if you want," I offered.

"Really?" Erin said, clearing her throat after another

cough. "That would be . . ." She paused and got a twinkle in her eyes. "Totally radical to the max, dude."

She cracked me up.

Later that night, I sat down at my desk and turned on my laptop. After doing the obstacle course with Erin, I kept thinking about how she'd said it was probably about input and output, like the sandwich exercise we'd done with Mrs. Clark. I thought I'd do some research to find out more.

A quick online search of the terms *input* and *output* for computers confirmed what Erin and I had talked about: A computer only does what it's told—and exactly what it's told—so if the directions you give it (the input) are terrible, the result (the output) will be terrible. *Ha!* Erin had totally nailed the connection between the playground exercise and Mrs. Clark's activity in coding club.

I found something else interesting: a term called GIGO, which was when you coded bad directions—it stood for "garbage in, garbage out." It sounded a lot like the "guy-go" sound Erin had made that I thought was part of her sneeze. If that was really what she was referring to, I wondered if she knew more about coding than I'd thought.

Either way, I finally felt like I was making some progress.

I might have failed the input/output exercise in coding club, but I did really well with the playground version of it. Maybe Alex really was helping me, after all!

I went downstairs and found Alex sitting at the kitchen counter next to Mom and Dad, all working on their laptops. Typical.

I came up behind Alex and hugged him tight.

"I can't breathe," he choked out, fake coughing a few times.

"Lucy, let go of your brother," Mom said distractedly.

I hugged Alex tighter. "Thank you!" I whispered.

"For what?" Alex said as I let go of him.

"You know what," I said, grinning. I hurried out of the kitchen and dashed up the stairs two at a time, back to my room.

Sometimes my brother could be really cool.

Chapter Seven

The next day, I woke up early. I wanted to see Alex before he left for school.

"Good morning!" I said as he sat with his cereal at the kitchen counter, reading his test prep study guide.

He kept eating.

"So, any fun plans for this beautiful day?" I asked.

He finally looked up at me. "Why are *you* in such a good mood?" He stared at me for a few seconds. "You've been acting kinda strange lately, Lu. You okay?"

"I'm totally fine. Actually, I'm not very busy today," I said, hinting that I'd be open to another coding activity. "So, what are *your* plans?"

He narrowed his eyes at me, and then decided to let it go. "School, then work," he said, putting his bowl in the sink and packing up his stuff.

Clearly, my brother was not ready to admit he was behind the coding notes, and I wasn't going to force him. I was fine letting him act like he had no clue what was going on. For now, at least.

"Cool. Are you stopping by to see Mrs. Clark at the middle school?" I asked.

"No," he said, tucking his laptop into his messenger bag. "Why would I do that?"

I put the milk away, not wanting to be too obvious. "Well, you were there yesterday . . ."

"I told you—I had to give her the recommendation form. And you didn't seem too thrilled to see me there, if I remember correctly." Alex raised one eyebrow. "You sure you're okay, Lu?"

"Of course I am."

"'Kay, well . . . I've got class. Gotta go."

We didn't usually leave at the same time, so I walked him to the door. "Maybe I'll see you later," I said. "You know where my school is . . ." Then I winked.

Alex looked at me as if I were nuts, and turned away.

In between classes that morning, I kept checking my

locker to see if something would show up, but nothing did. Maybe Alex really wasn't going to stop by the middle school today.

But after lunch, I saw an envelope taped to my locker. I opened it right away. The note inside read:

```
while (there_are_balls_left) {
    hit_the_ball ( );
}
```

Huh? I thought that after figuring out the first two notes, the next one would be easier. But this one was so weird! If it was about sports, what could it possibly have to do with coding? Was Alex trying to throw me off track?

Erin came by her locker, so I figured I'd see what she thought.

"Hey," I said. "Thanks again for helping me at the park yesterday."

She smiled, stacking her books in her locker. "No problem. It was fun."

"Look, I got another note." I handed her the letter. "What do you think it means?"

She studied it for a few seconds. "No idea," she said. "It's not like I know anything about coding," she added with an awkward smile.

I was confused. "But you seemed to know what the note at the park meant yesterday."

Erin's eyes shifted from side to side and she looked up and down the hall. Seeing that no one was within earshot, she leaned in toward me and whispered, "Yeah, I've been thinking. Don't tell anyone about that, okay?"

"About what?" I asked, confused.

"Exactly. Thanks," she answered. Then, raising her voice back to normal volume, she pointed at my note, adding, "Hitting balls . . . Maybe try going to one of the sports fields for clues?"

Seemed like a good idea. "I guess I could go after school." But I worried that Sophia would be there. I knew she was on the fields most days after school, either managing a team or practicing, and I didn't really want to talk to her. Things had become so awkward between us.

Then again, I knew I should go if I wanted to understand what the note meant. Maybe I didn't have to go alone, though.

"Do you want to come with me?" I asked Erin.

I could tell she was hesitating.

"You can use it as an excuse to get out of alphabetizing

books, or whatever your mom has planned for you today," I proposed.

"I'd love to, but sorry, I can't," she said, looking down at the books in her arms. "Yesterday was a one-time-only excuse. My mom'll get mad at me if I don't come home right after school today."

I was disappointed, but I understood. Maybe I could wrangle Anjali into coming along.

At lunch, Anjali told me she couldn't go with me—she had to babysit after school. I couldn't think of anyone else to ask, since everyone I knew had after-school activities. If I wanted to find out what the locker note meant, I was going to have to go to the sports fields on my own. I crossed my fingers and hoped that Sophia wouldn't be there.

After school, I headed to the fields with the latest locker note in hand.

I kept rereading it. *"While there are balls left, hit the ball."*

Hitting balls sounded like softball.

Maybe I was supposed to hit some balls to understand the note? I could start there. First, I was going to need a bat and a ball. It wasn't softball season, so I figured no one would mind if I used some of the equipment.

I headed toward the multipurpose sports field. There was a shed where sports equipment was kept, and it was usually open during practice times. I was halfway there when I saw Sophia standing in the batter's box, her back to the school's small row of bleachers. There were other teams and kids around, practicing for different sports. But Sophia was the only one on the softball part of the field.

I hung back for a few minutes, trying to figure out what to do. Sophia had a bucket of balls in front of her, and she was holding a bat. She picked a ball out of the bucket, threw it up into the air, and swung, over and over again. She'd hit the ball some of the time, but if the toss was just slightly off, she'd miss.

I didn't really want to talk to her, but there was no way to get to the shed without passing by her. Plus, I could tell how frustrating it was to toss balls to herself. And the few balls she managed to hit weren't going very far.

"Hey," I said, walking up to her. "How's it going?"

She eyed me suspiciously. "What are you doing here?"

"Just . . . some research," I answered, not wanting to explain the notes. "Looks like you're batting well," I said.

She dug the toe of her cleat into the grass. "Why would *you* care?"

I was getting fed up with how tense things were between us, especially now that we were in coding club together. It didn't used to be this way.

"Soph, I don't get what's going on. Why do you always have to be so mean to me?"

"*Me?*" she said, stunned. "*You're* one to talk!" She turned away and threw a ball up into the air. *Clang!* It didn't go very far.

"What are you *talking* about?!" I said, walking around the bucket so I was face-to-face with her. "When was I ever mean to you?"

She glared at me. "Um, I don't know, maybe when you totally *ditched* me last year." She almost spit in my face.

I stared at her, shocked. "Ditched *you*?" She was the one who had faded me out—not the other way around. I'd been upset about it for months, but had decided over the summer to let it go. It wasn't worth ruining sixth grade over someone who didn't want to be my friend anymore.

"We *used* to play sports together, remember?" She eyed me like I'd left part of my brain at home.

"Yeah, I remember," I said, thinking of how close we

used to be. We'd been best friends since preschool—until last year.

"Yeah, until you decided you were too good for sports—and me," Sophia said, her teeth clenched. She looked down at the bucket of balls.

Too good for her? I was starting to feel like there'd been a huge misunderstanding. "Soph, it wasn't about you. I just didn't want to do so many sports anymore. I thought you knew that." Sophia and I had always played a ton of sports together when we were little, and last year, I'd wanted to do different things they offered at school, like painting, cooking—even bowling. When I heard about coding club, I knew I had to try it out.

"Well, it seemed pretty clear that you didn't want to hang out with me anymore," she said, unrelenting.

"Soph, I *swear*, it had nothing to do with you. If I'd known that's what you thought, I would have said something sooner."

She tapped her bat against the bucket of softballs, not saying anything. I thought of all the fun we'd had the year before, like playing dress-up in my mom's old party clothes and making friendship bracelets at her house. We'd even played a prank on my brother—we'd replaced the frosting in Oreos with toothpaste, and he'd fallen for it!

"Soph," I said gently, realizing how we'd both completely misinterpreted what had happened between us. "C'mon. You've got to believe me. Are you really going to let a stupid sports thing mean we can't be friends? I swear it had nothing to do with you."

She stopped tapping her bat against the bucket. "I just wish you'd told me what you were doing, you know? It's like you just disappeared. For no reason."

I could tell I had really hurt her. "I'm sorry, Soph. But you could've talked to me about it, too . . ."

"I know . . ." Her tone softened. "It really wasn't because you didn't want to be friends anymore?"

"Of *course* not. I always wanted . . ." I paused, putting my hand on her arm. "I *want* to be friends with you."

She looked hesitant.

"Soph," I said. "For old times' sake, let me toss you the ball."

She smiled, and I could feel the tension between us loosening.

"Wait, why are you here, anyway?" she asked. "Did you come here just to talk to me?"

I figured I might as well tell her all about the notes. She'd known Alex her whole life, so I knew she'd understand.

I told her about the first two notes and explained why learning to code fast was so important to me.

"Here's the latest one," I said, handing it to her.

"*While there are balls left, hit the ball*," Sophia read out loud. "That's just like Alex to be so mysterious."

"I know, right?" I said. It was nice to talk with someone who knew him so well.

Sophia bent down and picked up a ball. She tossed it to me. "We still have a ball, so why not hit it—let's see if you can still throw!" she said with a smirk.

It took me about three terrible throws to get back into it. Sophia didn't hit it out of the park, but she hit the balls farther than when she was on her own.

We quickly emptied the bucket of balls.

"*While there are balls left, hit the ball*," Sophia repeated while we gathered the balls and refilled the bucket.

"Thing is, if we keep picking up the balls, there's always going to be a ball to hit. We'll never run out," I told Sophia. "That's what doesn't make sense about the note." I pointed to the now full bucket. "And what does this have to do with coding, anyway?"

"I guess as long as we can, we keep going," Sophia said.

"Maybe it's about how computers keep on going, as long as they're charged?"

"Maybe." I felt like there should be more to it. And when should we stop? My arm was getting tired.

After a few more throws, with the best crack of a bat that I had ever heard, Sophia hit the ball across the field.

"Awesome, Soph! Home run!" I cheered. She held her bat up in the air, cheering.

From that moment on, Soph was on fire. I got into it, too, changing things up and making her work a little harder. She didn't miss a single pitch.

We gathered balls a few more times until we were both exhausted. The sun was setting behind the bleachers, and other school teams were packing up and heading to the lockers.

I jogged from the pitcher's mound to Sophia. "I think we should call it a day."

"Yeah, you're right. But your note says *'While there are balls left, hit the ball.'*"

"But there's never going to be an end," I said, rubbing my shoulder. "This could go on and on forever."

"Maybe that's the point?" Sophia said, glancing down at a blister that had popped up on her right hand. She turned to show me the red mark. "Like how you can keep playing a video game until you run out of lives or time?" I shrugged. "How 'bout this," she continued. "Let's put the equipment away and try to figure out the coding connection."

"Good idea," I said. Once the balls and bat were back in the shed, we sat in the bleachers and looked stuff up on our phones, but nothing made the connection clear.

"I wish Alex would just tell me what it means," I said, getting frustrated.

"Why don't I come over to your place?" Sophia suggested. She lived just a block over from me. "Maybe he'll be there, and we can ask him."

"We could, but he hasn't let his guard down about the notes yet," I told her. "I doubt he will now."

"Yeah, but it can't hurt to try, right?" Sophia said.

She was right.

"Want to ask your *abuela* if you can stay for dinner?" I said. Sophia had three little sisters, and her mom worked the night shift at the hospital. Her dad was a real estate agent and could get really busy. So her grandmother moved in with them last year from Puerto Rico to help out. "We can corner Alex and force him to explain what this all means."

"Sounds great!"

It was starting to feel like things were back to normal between Soph and me. I realized how much I'd missed her this past year. All because of a stupid misunderstanding!

As luck would have it, Alex never showed up for dinner. He didn't answer my calls or texts, either. I knew he was busy with his girlfriend and college stuff, but I wished he'd at least respond to me.

My mom was still at work, so Soph and I ate dinner with my dad. He was glad to see that Soph and I were talking again, and peppered her with questions about her summer. After dessert, Soph and I tried to search online again for the connection between hitting softballs and coding. We even looked through some of my mom's coding books, but we couldn't find anything. After a while, we gave up and took silly selfies together instead.

It felt like no time had passed at all since we'd stopped hanging out.

Chapter Eight

*T*hursday morning, I rushed into school, fully expecting to find a note on my locker. Alex had left home earlier than usual, saying there was something he "had to do."

When I got to my locker, there it was—a note taped to the door—just as I expected.

As confusing as the ball-playing note was (I was still annoyed about not understanding what it meant), this one was worse.

It said:

```
int number_of_buttons = 1  2  3  4  5  6  7  8;
string button_type = "_____";
boolean has_sleeves = true  false;
string sleeve_type = "_____";
```

```
string collar_type = "_____";
string lace_type = "_____";
```

I considered texting Alex and asking, "What the heck?!" But since he hadn't answered any of my texts or calls the day before, I decided not to bother. Besides, he would have acted like he didn't know anything, anyway.

If I couldn't figure this one out myself, I'd have two notes to talk to him about at dinner tonight!

As I turned the corner, I saw Sophia walking down the hall with a huge pile of textbooks in her arms. They were stacked up past her head, and she was shouting, "Out of the way!" to the other kids in the hall.

I stepped up next to her, where she could see me from the side.

"Soph, what are you doing?"

"Ugh," she grunted. One of the books at the top of the pile teetered. I grabbed it before it fell. "I went to the office to get the athlete health forms for my parents to sign so I can try out for the softball team . . ." She paused and said, "Thanks for helping me practice yesterday, by the way."

"You're welcome," I told her. "Any time."

"I was about to leave the office when Principal Stephens

asked if I was going by the library. He wanted me to return a few books."

"A few?" I grabbed another book from the top of her stack. "This is more than a few!"

"I know." She shifted her weight to keep the pile even. "He was laughing when he added the last one to the top."

We had time before class, and I was headed past the library, too. "Let me help," I said, taking another couple of books and adding them to my pile.

"Thanks, Lu. You're a good friend." Sophia smiled at me. "I mean that."

"You're a good friend, too, Soph," I said, smiling back.

When we got to the library, we dropped off the books on the librarian's desk.

"So, I got a new note," I told Sophia as the librarian scanned the books.

"Really? What'd it say?" I handed her Alex's strange lesson for the day.

"Boo-le-an? String? Type?" Sophia scrunched her face. "I don't get it. Did you text Alex?"

I shook my head. "There's no point. And I want to try to solve this one on my own," I told her. We walked out the library's large glass doors and into the hall.

"Maybe we could ask Maya about it," Sophia suggested. "Button, lace, collar—she's into fashion and she's in coding club, so she might have an idea of what it all means."

"I—" Talking to Maya wasn't really on my list of things I wanted to do. I hardly knew her, and for some reason I got nervous talking to her. We'd barely said a word when we made Sophia's sandwich during coding club.

Soph could tell what I was thinking. She put a hand on my shoulder. "I can ask her for you, if you want," she said. "My locker is next to hers and I see her all the time."

"I don't know . . ."

"I think she's our best bet for solving this one, Lu."

"Okay," I said eventually, grateful for her offer. "But let's ask her together." I was the one getting the notes, and I didn't want Sophia to have to do the work for me.

We agreed that Sophia would ask Maya if we could talk at lunch.

At lunch, I sat with Anjali—for once she wasn't doing extra work for film club.

"Sorry for being so MIA with film," she said. "This week has been crazy. But I want to hear all about the new club. And what's going on with the coding thing?" she said, taking a bite of her apple. "Are Alex's notes helping you? Do you still need me to figure out how to fast-track you?"

I told her about Alex's latest notes. "I did learn something after the playground thing," I said. "But I have no idea about the other ones. And I still haven't learned enough to get started on my app."

She took out a granola bar. "Hmm . . . that is annoying. But, Lucy, I really think Alex is trying to help you."

"Yeah, maybe," I answered after taking a bite of my tuna sandwich. I was still unsure the notes were actually helping, but figured it was worth a try. Plus, it'd been fun getting to know Erin at the playground and hitting balls with Sophia on the softball field.

I saw Sophia at the end of the lunch line and waved at her. She came over and plopped her tray next to mine.

"Hey, Soph!" Anjali said. She looked back and forth between us. "Wait, are you guys talking again? I thought that was, like, not allowed."

Sophia and I smiled at each other.

I reached for my milk carton. "Yeah, we're good now," I said to Anjali. "Sophia realized how stupid she was being,"

"Hey!" Sophia said, elbowing me. I elbowed her back, giggling.

"Um, okay, not sure what's going on here, but I like it!" Anjali said. "Hey, did you guys hear about Erin?"

"No," I said, realizing I hadn't seen Erin by our lockers all day.

"She went home sick. She wasn't feeling well in Spanish class so Señora Martinez let her go to the nurse, but she came back to get her things and went home. She had a fever, apparently."

"That sucks," I said.

"I told her we'd text her tonight to see how she's doing."

Of course—leave it to Anjali to reach out to the new girl. She was doing what she did best—being the nicest person in school.

"Group chat?" I asked her.

"Let's do it!" Anjali said. "Want to be in on it, Sophia? You know Erin from coding club, right?"

"Sure!" Sophia said.

I saw Maya approaching our table from behind Sophia, and instinctively got nervous about what I was wearing. I didn't know why I got so self-conscious around Maya—it's not like I cared *that* much about clothes.

I looked down at my outfit. Black skinny jeans with a white sweater and my jean jacket. Okay, that wasn't so bad. My shoes were the problem—I was wearing scruffy old sneakers. I tried to hide my feet under the lunch table, hoping she wouldn't notice.

Maya was wearing boots with a full patchwork skirt and bright yellow blouse. As usual, she looked amazing.

"Hey, guys," she said, taking a seat next to Sophia. "Lucy, Sophia told me you had a question," she said to me. "What's up?"

"Oh yeah . . . thanks . . . um . . . for helping!" I stammered. Ugh, why was I so embarrassing! I reached into my jacket pocket, where I was now collecting all the notes.

"I told my brother I wanted to learn how to code, and I'm pretty sure he's been leaving me these weird notes at my locker."

I handed Maya the pieces of paper.

"Lucy's been trying to figure out what they mean," Sophia explained. She pointed to the latest note. "Since this one has clothing stuff on it, we thought maybe you'd have some ideas."

Maya looked it over, her eyebrows furrowed. She thumbed through the other notes, too.

"Have you figured out what these other ones mean?" she asked, looking up at us.

"Well, kind of," I said. "I went to the playground with Erin—the new girl—on Tuesday after school, and we followed the instructions on the first note. We're pretty sure it's about the input/output stuff we learned in coding club on Monday."

"Except that you actually gave decent instructions this time," Sophia said teasingly. She pointed to the second note. "Yesterday, Lucy and I hit softballs to try to figure this one out, but we got nowhere."

After a long pause, Maya said, "Lucy, are you sure it's your brother who's behind all this?"

"Pretty sure," I answered. Anjali and Sophia nodded in agreement. "Why?"

"Well, I don't know him, but I think whoever wrote this note knows me," she said, handing the third note back to me.

"What?" I was confused. "What do you mean?"

"I'll show you," Maya said. "Can you come to Dress to Impress after school?"

"The designer clothes place?" Anjali asked. "Why there?"

"I help out at the store sometimes." She looked at me. "There's something I want to show you."

"I can go with you, if you want," Sophia offered. "I don't have to be at practice today till later. And I'm curious about the note, too."

This was turning out to be an even more interesting day than I'd anticipated.

Dress to Impress specialized in designer wedding dresses, but also custom-made tuxedos and party dresses. If someone needed a dress hemmed or a fancy button replaced, the shop was the place to go for that, too. I'd never been there, but I knew my mom had gone to get clothes fixed for special occasions.

After school, Sophia and I followed directions to the store from my phone. When we walked by the new computer place, I couldn't help glancing at the newest models in the window. I loved trying to pick the one I'd get if I could buy a new one—not that that would happen anytime soon. In the meantime, at least I got to inherit Alex's and my parents' hand-me-downs.

I got a glimpse of a few new laptops in cool colors, like metallic pink and gold. But what caught my eye was a flyer taped to the window.

CALLING ALL CODERS!

Don't miss the six-hour hackathon for middle-schoolers at the community center on October 28! Some beginner coding knowledge required. Includes a $100 prize!

COME PREPARED TO BUILD FOR THE FUTURE!

Sophia had stopped to take a look, too. "What do you think a hackathon is?" I asked her.

"No clue," Sophia said, checking the time on her phone. "C'mon, I gotta get back before the end of football practice. Let's go!"

There were some flyers in a basket, so I took one and put it in my jean jacket pocket.

When we got to Dress to Impress, Maya was sitting on a tall stool at the front counter, sewing a button on a silky yellow dress.

After our conversation at lunch, I was feeling more comfortable around her. She hadn't seemed to notice my scruffy sneakers—and if she had, they didn't appear to bother her. I was relieved to think she wouldn't judge me for my clothes.

"Hey," I said. "Cool place." The window display was set up like a school dance scene with a boy mannequin and girl mannequin standing together. The girl's dress was beautiful; it was teal and white with a low back and long puffy skirt. The guy had a basic black tux, with a teal tie that matched his date's dress.

"Thanks," Maya said, gathering her stuff. "Come in. Did you bring the note?"

I reached in my jacket pocket where I was collecting all the notes, and took out the latest one. "Yep."

"Great." She opened a door to the back of the shop and led us to a workroom. There were stacks of fabric piled between a rack of partially finished clothing and two sewing machines. I saw bins along the wall that were labeled "lace" and "buttons," plus other things I didn't recognize, like "tulle."

"This is what I wanted to show you." From the corner of the room, she brought out one of those mannequins without a head that professional designers use. It had on a gorgeous, shimmery green dress that looked half-finished. "Friends of my mom own this store, and when I help out, they let me use their supplies for my own projects. I've been working on this dress for a while—I usually leave it out front, but I thought I'd bring it back here to show you guys," Maya said. "I've already asked Principal Stephens if I can show it at the school's spring talent show."

"Wow, it's so pretty!" I said, moving in to take a closer look. "I didn't know you were into making clothes."

"This is so amazing," Sophia said, reaching out to touch the fabric.

It wasn't done, but what she'd finished was incredible. The green material shimmered with purple swirls, like someone had mixed two paints, but not blended them all the way. The skirt ruffled around the waist with an Asian floral print down one side. I could imagine Maya wearing this dress, not just to the talent show, but to the middle-school spring dance. She'd definitely have the best dress there.

"But wait, what do you think your dress has to do with the note I got?" I asked.

She turned the mannequin so that Sophia and I could

look at it together. "I'll show you. There are some major decisions I need to make at this point." She paused as if challenging us to guess what those were.

"Buttons?" Sophia pointed to where tiny buttons could go down the front.

"Sleeves?" I asked. There were none yet.

Maya was waiting for us to say more, but we were stumped.

"Look at the note you got, Lucy," Maya said. I read the note in my hand.

```
int number_of_buttons = 1  2  3  4  5  6  7  8;
string button_type = "_____";
boolean has_sleeves =  true  false;
string sleeve_type = "_____";
string collar_type = "_____";
string lace_type = "_____";
```

"Collar," Sophia said. It was no longer a question.

I finished the list. "And lace!" I could see where Maya could add lace on the skirt, or on the top part of the dress.

"Exactly," Maya said. "Those happen to be the four things I've been planning to add to my dress. Whoever wrote this note seemed to know that, and I highly doubt that's your brother, Lucy."

"That *is* really weird," I said, letting it all sink in. "But what does this even mean for coding?"

"I'm less curious about what it means," Maya said, "than about *who* knew those were the decisions I needed to make."

"Maybe it was a coincidence," Sophia suggested.

Maya shook her head. "It can't be," she said. "The similarities are just too obvious."

"Who's come to the shop recently?" I asked.

"A lot of people," Maya said. "Let me think . . . A bunch of kids from school, their parents, some teachers . . . Not your brother, though. I've never seen him here."

"Maybe he was here getting a suit for prom or graduation? He might have come when you weren't here," I suggested, but as I said it, I knew it was impossible. One, he wasn't a suit kind of guy. And two, those events were months away. Alex wasn't the type to plan past lunch.

"I checked all the recent receipts. His name isn't on one," Maya told us. "But lots of other people from school came in. This past week, I saw the new eighth-grade science teacher and a bunch of teachers from the seventh grade. They're having some kind of fancy staff banquet. Principal Stephens was also here."

There didn't seem to be any clear clues about who could have known what Maya was planning for her dress, and then left me a note about it.

"I know!" Maya suddenly said, standing up. She brought down four bins from the shelves. Each was labeled: Buttons. Lace. Collars. Sleeves.

"It looks like we're supposed to fill out the note, right?" she said as she took the lids off the boxes. We nodded. "So why not do that? Maybe it'll give us a clue. Buttons first." Maya dumped out hundreds of buttons on the table. There were big ones and little ones. Plastic, metal, wood, and pearl—buttons in every color of the rainbow.

Maya handed me a pen. "Lucy, write down our choices on the note's blank lines."

"Are you sure this is what we're supposed to do?" I asked.

"No," Maya admitted. "But it's all I can think of, and besides, if it's wrong, at least you'll have helped me make decisions for my dress," she said, smiling.

Sophia and I looked at each other and shrugged. Maya was right. Might as well fill out the note as best as we could. What was there to lose?

Chapter Nine

That night, Sophia and I group chatted with Erin. Anjali was supposed to join us, but she got busy with family stuff.

E: ah yes plz! but we don't have all our classes together . . . 😩 😩 😩

L: oh yeah forgot we're not in the same grade lol! 😩 😩 😩 😩

S: haha lets ask maya to help shes in 7grade too

L: yay great idea! 👍 👍 👍

After our afternoon with Maya at Dress to Impress, we'd exchanged numbers in case anything else came up about the coding notes, so we added her to the chat.

Maya texted back right away.

M: happy to help! 🙂 🙂 🙂

We decided we'd all go over to Erin's house on Saturday to bring her homework. I hoped she'd feel better by then.

On Friday morning, Sophia and I were walking down the hall to English class when we heard a voice behind us.

"Lucy! Sophia!"

"Hey, Maya!" I answered as she caught up to us. I didn't feel nervous around her anymore, especially after hanging out the day before. She was much more laid-back and fun than I'd thought.

"Cute earrings," she said, noticing my heart studs.

I instinctively touched one of my earlobes. "Thanks!"

"So listen," she said, leaning in and lowering her voice as we walked down the hallway. "I have an idea for how to find the note-leaver."

Even though we hadn't figured out how—or even if—Alex could have seen Maya's dress, I was still convinced the notes were from him. It was entirely possible that he'd come up with buttons, sleeves, collars, and lace on his own, and that the similarities to Maya's dress were just a weird coincidence. Still, I was glad it'd given me the chance to hang out with Maya and Sophia. But I also didn't want to waste time following wrong leads.

"I'm telling you, Maya, if it doesn't involve cornering my brother, I really don't think it's worth it," I said. Sophia nodded in agreement.

"I know you think the notes are from him, Lucy. But what if they're not?" Maya insisted. "Aren't you just a bit curious who else they could be from?"

I could tell she was excited about whatever idea she had brewing.

"Okay, what's your idea?" I conceded.

Maya grinned. "If you don't get another note on your locker today, we use our answers to the dress note as bait."

"Bait? What are you talking about?" Sophia asked, her head tilted.

Maya's eyes lit up. "Simple: We leave the filled-out note on Lucy's locker and see if the culprit shows up to take it."

I could see where she was going with this. All three of us looked at one another and smiled.

"Let's do it!" I said.

Later that day, I still hadn't received a new note on my locker, so we taped the one with our dress-making answers on it to my locker door in between classes. It was right after fifth period, when we had a bit longer than usual before the bell would ring. I'd made a copy of the note, just so we'd have one in case the one on my locker fell or something.

Our filled-out portion of the note said:

```
int number_of_buttons = 1  2  3  4  5 ⑥ 7  8;
string button_type = "purple seed pearl";
boolean has_sleeves = (true) false;
string sleeve_type = "Petal";
string collar_type = "Mandarin";
string lace_type = "Antique Chinese Jacquard";
```

"Now we just need a place where we can watch your locker in secret," Maya said, trying to look around discreetly. We realized there was one spot where we could watch my locker and be hidden: the girls' bathroom across the hall. We went in and took turns peeking out the door to look for anyone who might take the note.

"Bradley Steinberg is standing nearby," Maya said after just a minute. Sophia and I smushed up next to her to look out.

"It can't be him," I said. "We talked about coding club at lunch the other day, and it was pretty clear he knows nothing about coding."

I turned around and leaned against the wall. Maya walked toward the mirrors, deep in thought.

"What about Erin?" Maya finally said, turning to me and Sophia.

"Erin?" I answered, incredulous.

"Does she even know any coding?" Sophia asked, turning around for a second. She was standing guard with the bathroom door cracked open.

"I think a little," I said. I flashed back to how Erin had asked me not to tell anyone about what she'd said in the playground.

"Think about it, Lucy. Could Erin be the one leaving the notes?" Maya probed.

"But she wasn't even in school yesterday," I said.

"She was in the morning," Sophia reminded me, her eyes glued to my locker again. "She left during Spanish class."

I had to admit there were clues that seemed to point Erin's way, but why would she want to show me how to code through secret notes? If she wanted to help me, she could just be open about it.

"No," I said. "It can't be Erin. It doesn't add up." I turned and peeked out the door with Sophia. "Any other suspects?"

"Sammy Cooper, Ellie Foster, and Alicia Lee from coding club are in the hallway," Sophia said. "But they aren't near your locker."

The warning bell rang. "Mrs. Clark just walked by," Sophia reported.

"Did she take the note?" Maya asked. She was at the mirror, retying a bow on her blouse.

"No," Sophia said. "She was talking to the Spanish teacher—watch out!"

The bathroom door flew open. Sophia jumped back so fast, she almost knocked me down.

A few kids from eighth grade walked in. We pretended we were busy fixing our hair until they left.

"Phew, close call!" Sophia said, taking up guard at the door again as soon as they were gone.

I couldn't get my mind off Maya suggesting that Erin was the culprit. It occurred to me that since Maya was in seventh grade, she could have been in coding club the year before, and we wouldn't know it. Maybe *she* was the note-leaver, and her helping us was a cover-up! But why would she go through the trouble of writing anonymous notes? It didn't really make sense.

Still, I had to ask. "Maya, do *you* already know how to code?"

She was now touching up her eyeliner. "What?" she said.

"Well, you're the one who said we should consider other suspects . . . ," I explained.

She looked back at me incredulously, her eyeliner in midair. "Wait, are you accusing *me* of writing the notes? Why would I pretend not to know about them? And why would I have invited you guys to Dress to Impress?" she said, her voice rising.

I had to agree, it didn't really add up.

"Sorry, I just thought . . ."

"Whatever," she said tersely, throwing her eyeliner into her backpack. "Forget it. It's not like I even care about coding. I don't know why I was trying to help you."

I hadn't meant to offend her, but now she was going too far. "Then why are you in coding club if you don't even care about coding?" I asked, hands on my waist.

She slung her backpack over her shoulder, averting her eyes.

"Well, what is it?" Sophia asked her. She'd stopped guarding the door and was at the mirror now, too.

Maya looked uncomfortable. "Fine," she finally said with a sigh. "I was sent there. The school paper assigned us to write articles about some of the school clubs. I wasn't at the meeting when they made the assignments, so I got the club that still had room."

I couldn't believe it. "Wait . . . so you're, like . . . undercover?"

Maya scoffed. "Ha! That makes it sound way more glamorous than it is," she said, adjusting her backpack. "I only need to stay for a few sessions for the article. Mrs. Clark knows that I'm supposed to be leaving." She started for the door, then turned around.

"But I have to admit, it's been fun hanging out with you guys. Thanks for helping me with my dress yesterday."

I decided I didn't want to argue about this anymore. It just wasn't worth it. "Wait, Maya, don't go," I said, grabbing her arm. "I'm sorry I accused you. Let's just forget about it, okay?"

I suddenly realized that we'd been talking and no one had been watching my locker door.

"The note!" I screeched.

I dashed out into the hallway.

The note was gone.

Chapter Ten

*A*s much fun as I was having hanging out with Sophia, Maya, and Erin, by Friday night, I was beginning to have doubts about whether or not my brother really was behind the coding notes. We hadn't found any definitive evidence against him, but we hadn't figured out who else it could be, either.

I went to the kitchen, figuring I'd sit there as long as it took to catch him on his way in. I needed to talk to him, and a sneak attack might be the only way to get the job done.

To my surprise, Alex was sitting at the counter, working on his laptop.

I went up next to him and put my elbow on the counter. "Alex, if you're the one leaving me notes, you've got to tell me."

He looked at me like I had an extra eye on my forehead.

"What are you talking about, Lu?" he said, his brow wrinkled.

I contemplated my options. I could push it, but was it even worth it? It wasn't like he was going to admit the notes were from him—he clearly wasn't willing to back down from this prank.

"Forget it," I said, plopping onto a stool next to him. "I just wish I could help make my app for Uncle Mickey faster, that's all."

"Lu, you know you don't need an app to show Uncle Mickey how much you care. Why don't you call or visit him? I'm sure he'd appreciate it."

I knew he was right, but still, I felt helpless.

Alex's phone rang. I could tell something was wrong when he answered, because he kept saying, "Uh-huh, uh-huh," and quickly got up to get his jacket and wallet.

"The late-shift delivery driver's sick," he said to me as he hung up and headed toward the door. "See ya!"

Oh well, I was glad I'd at least had a chance to chat with him, even if briefly.

After Alex left, I couldn't stop thinking about Maya not believing that Alex was the one leaving the notes. Maybe she was right. But who could it be instead? I knew Maya thought Erin could be the culprit, but Erin wasn't at school Friday when the dress-making note disappeared from my locker. It had to be someone who was at school that day.

Unless a random person took the note off my locker? Anything was possible, at this point.

My mom came into the kitchen and told me that Dad would be home with pizza soon. I sat on the couch and texted Anjali a bit, and then watched TV. It was actually nice to have some quiet time to myself.

Saturday morning, I was glad that we'd made plans to meet at Erin's house, even just to get my mind off the notes. I met Sophia and Maya outside Erin's building. The apartment complex was an older one—some of the paint was peeling on the front, but there was a pool out back with a slide.

We walked up to Erin's apartment and rang the bell.

"Good morning," a woman greeted us. She was wearing dust-covered sweatpants, and her short blond hair spiked up a little on top. "I'm Suzie, Erin's mom. You must be Erin's new friends."

"Hi. I'm Lucy, this is Sophia, and this is Maya," I said as

Soph and Maya smiled at Erin's mom.

"It's nice to meet you all. Come in."

Inside Erin's apartment, there were boxes stacked everywhere, and books and clothes strewn all over the floor.

"I'm so sorry for the mess," Suzie said bashfully. "You can just walk over anything." She pushed some boxes out of the way.

"We'd be happy to help you and Erin unpack," Maya offered.

"That's so sweet of you, but we're almost done," she said. She pointed toward the back. "Erin's in the kitchen."

When we walked into the kitchen, Erin was standing at the counter with a mixing bowl in front of her. She was wearing an apron and had white flecks of flour in her hair.

"Hi, guys!" she said. She dusted her hands off on her apron. "Thanks so much for coming over. Ignore the mess—we're still unpacking, but I wanted to do a little baking."

Sophia took a deep breath. "Smells amazing in here!"

"It's just cookies in the oven," Erin said. "They'll be done soon. We can have some, if you want."

"I'm always in the mood for cookies," I said. "Looks like you're feeling better, Erin!"

"I am," she answered, taking off her apron.

Maya handed her a packet. "Special delivery."

"Oh, thanks! I wish there was a better way to get homework." She put the papers on a clean counter. "I checked online, but not everything is posted, and there aren't any class notes."

"Yeah, it's not the best system," Sophia said.

The oven timer rang, and Erin grabbed oven mitts to take out the cookies. She put a few on a plate.

"Here, have some," she said, handing us each a couple of warm cookies on a paper towel. "Careful, they're hot."

I let mine cool a bit and took a bite. It was sweet, gooey, and soft, all at once.

"Mmmm, these are so good!" I said, my mouth full. "What's in them?"

"White chocolate chips and dried raspberries," Erin said, putting more cookies on the plate.

"Yum! How did you learn to make these?" Sophia asked her, finishing hers in two bites.

Erin pointed to a shelf full of old, frayed-looking books.

"I used a recipe from an old cookbook," she said. "I collect them."

"Really?" I said, my mouth still full.

"Yeah, I love looking at the pictures and being able to turn the pages. It's different than looking at a website or blog."

"Delish!" Maya said, licking crumbs off her lips and fingers. "You've got talent, girl!"

Erin's mom popped her head into the kitchen. "Isn't my baby an amazing baker?" she said, looking adoringly at her daughter. She put an arm around Erin. "I'm so glad she met you girls. It's always tough for her to make friends at a new school."

"Mom!" Erin groaned.

"Is that TMI? Sorry, honey."

"Definitely," Erin said, her face reddening. "TMI."

Erin's mom's cell phone rang, and she shuffled around the kitchen until she found it in the mess of boxes. "I'll let you girls bond without an embarrassing mom around," she said, giving Erin a peck before leaving with her phone.

"Ugh." Erin's face flushed. "Moms . . ."

"Don't worry. Mine's a total nerd," I said. "She plays video games for hours. The way she yells at the screen like my brother, you'd think she was still in high school."

"Yeah, you have nothing to worry about. My parents love ballroom dancing," Maya told us. "They practice in the living room—while I have friends over!"

We all giggled, imagining the scene.

"My mom thinks she's really good at voices, but she's actually terrible at them," Sophia added.

"So true!" I said, laughing. I'd heard lots of Sophia's mom's "voices," and they were all pretty bad.

"Erin's actually great at voices," I said, remembering her funny imitation at the playground the other day. "Do your French one, Erin!" I said. But the second I said it and saw Erin's expression, I wished I hadn't.

"Oops. Sorry!" I hadn't realized that maybe she didn't want it to be public knowledge.

"It's okay," Erin said, her face relaxing. She suddenly became the actress I'd seen in the park. In a perfect Dracula imitation, she raised her hands as if to strangle me and growled, "I vill make you pay . . ."

We all chuckled.

"As long as we're spilling secrets," Maya interrupted. She turned to Erin. "Tell us: Are *you* the mystery coder leaving notes for Lucy?"

I couldn't believe Maya was being so blunt. Erin looked horrified, and her face went pale. "Who told you I know coding?" she asked.

All eyes turned to me.

"I'm so sorry!" I said, my eyes wide. "I know you asked me not to tell people about the playground, but it seemed like you knew stuff about coding, and you said GIGO, and we're still trying to figure out who's leaving me those notes . . ."

"What's guy-go?" Maya asked.

"Garbage in, garbage out," Erin and I said together.

"It's what happens when you give a computer bad input," I explained. "I looked it up."

Now I was starting to get suspicious, too. "Wait, Erin, *do* you know how to code?" I said, turning to her.

She looked down at her apron, and then up at us. "Okay, I admit I know a bit about coding," she confessed. "It's fun, but I don't want to do it anymore. And no, I'm not leaving you the notes. Did you guys *really* think it was me?"

"Well, we wondered . . . ," Sophia admitted.

"Hold on a second, so you *do* know how to code?" Maya asked, glancing at me with an "I told you so" face. "How'd you learn? And why are you in coding club?"

"Oh, it's a long story," Erin said, waving her hand dismissively. I could tell she didn't think we'd be interested.

"We want to hear it, right, guys?" Maya said, looking at me and Sophia. We nodded.

"Okay . . . ," Erin said, reluctantly. "My dad's in the military. That's why we've moved so much. When he'd get transferred, we'd all go. Now my parents are getting divorced, so Mom and I came to live near my aunt." She pulled a coding textbook out of a box of cookbooks on the counter. "My dad's really into coding, so he's been teaching me for the past few years. When we moved here, I wanted to join the theater club, but there weren't any spots open. My mom insisted that I do coding, since my dad's not around to teach me as much anymore. She says it's a practical skill, and she wants me to keep it up." Erin looked down at the coding book, her face drawn. "I like coding, but it just reminds me of my dad too much. I'd rather sing and dance."

She looked so sad, I felt bad for her. "But think of the bright side—you got to meet us!" I said, trying to cheer her up.

"I know," she said. "I just wish I could try something different." Under her breath, she added, "Last year, I got a spot in the talent show at my old school. I loved it. But other than that, I've never gotten to act or sing—well, except in my living room."

I thought about the tears Erin had on her face when she came to coding club last week. She must have been upset about not getting a chance to do theater.

"But I have something to tell you guys," Erin continued after a pause. "Last night, Principal Stephens called my mom and told her I could be in theater club starting next Monday if I wanted to—a spot opened up!"

"And your mom's letting you?" Maya said.

Erin nodded. "I told her why I'd rather do theater, and she agreed to let me try. I think she feels guilty about the move."

"Wait," I said, realizing what was happening. "So you're leaving coding club?"

"Well, it looks like it . . . ," Erin answered slowly.

"But you're the only one in our group who knows anything about coding," I said. She was our best chance to figure out the notes. "We need you!"

"Oh, you guys'll be fine without me," Erin answered. "And I already agreed to switch anyway." Seeing my face fall, she added, "If you want, I can explain the activities you've been doing. Have you gotten more notes, Lucy?"

I liked hanging out with Erin, and I didn't want her to leave the club. But I also didn't want to lose a chance to solve the coding notes mystery.

"I have," I said, taking them out of my jean jacket. I took them everywhere I went now. "Here's one about hitting balls that doesn't make any sense."

Sophia chimed in. "Lucy and I followed the instructions and hit baseballs for a while, but we couldn't figure out what it meant."

I pointed to the latest note. "This one is about clothes, so we went to Dress to Impress and filled it out based on a dress Maya's making." I showed her the copy I'd made, since the one on the locker had been taken.

"But we have no idea what it means for coding," Maya added.

Erin looked at the two notes and grabbed a piece of paper. We all huddled around her at the kitchen counter. She wrote down four things:

Input/Output
Conditionals
Loops
Variables

Maya eyed her suspiciously. "Are you *sure* you didn't write the notes?" she asked.

"I promise—it wasn't me," Erin said. "You guys get input/output, right?" She pointed to it on the list.

"Yeah," I answered. "The computer needs clear directions. It only does what it's told. Just like Mrs. Clark couldn't make a sandwich without us telling her exactly how, and like you couldn't get around the obstacle course in the playground unless I told you what to do."

"Exactly." Erin gave me a thumbs-up. "We also learned conditionals at the park, Lucy," she said.

I still had the first two notes, so I laid them out on the counter with the others.

"What do the curly squiggles and parentheses mean?" Maya asked, looking it over.

"The squiggles are called curly brackets," Erin explained. "They're an important part of some programming languages. They help the computer interpret your code. Sometimes code doesn't work just because it's missing a single bracket. And every programming language has a different syntax."

"Syntax?" I asked.

"Yeah, the way words and phrases are put together to

make up a language," Erin explained. "All languages, like English or Spanish, have their own syntax, just like coding does."

So far, this all made sense to me.

Erin pointed to the first note:

```
if (you_want_to_learn_code) {
    do_everything_I_tell_you ( );
}
```

"These lines of code are if statements, or conditionals," Erin explained. "*If* the first conditions are met, *then* the directions will be followed by a computer."

Maya gave her a confused look.

"See, in the first line the parentheses contain the condition for the if statement," Erin continued. "*If* you want to learn to code, *then* do what it says. The second line is a function—like an instruction—and the parentheses tell the computer to *run* the code."

"Oh, I get it. So the first note was my first conditional, or if statement," I said. "And the second note had conditionals, too." I pointed to the note about the playground:

```
if (you_agree_to_my_terms) {
    grab_a_friend ( );
```

```
    go_to_school_playground ( );
}
if (you_go_to_school_playground) {
    look_under_benches ( );
    find_a_big_yellow_envelope ( );
}
if (you_find_the_envelope) {
    trust_me ("You will learn to code");
}
```

"Exactly," Erin said.

"Okay, I understand conditionals," Sophia said. "But what about the sports note?" She pointed to it. "Does that have anything to do with coding?"

```
while (there_are_balls_left) {
    hit_the_ball ( );
}
```

"Loops," Erin said. "Loops are actions that you perform while a condition is still true."

"The softballs," Sophia said, connecting the dots. "When we didn't have a ball left," Sophia reasoned, "we would have had to stop."

"Only then," Erin said. "Otherwise it's the softball practice that never ends. You'd be caught in a loop."

"Ha! Well, we did get tired from throwing and hitting the balls," I said, rubbing my pitching arm, which was still sore.

"Yeah," Erin said, leaning back against the counter. "You're human. But computers never get tired of doing the same things over and over again . . . even if it's a million times. That's why loops are so great."

"And what about the note with the clothing stuff?" Maya said.

We looked at the filled-out note:

```
int number_of_buttons = 1 2 3 4 5 ⑥ 7 8;
string button_type = "purple seed pearl";
boolean has_sleeves = ⟨true⟩ false;
string sleeve_type = "Petal";
string collar_type = "Mandarin";
string lace_type = "Antique Chinese Jacquard";
```

"You guys filled this out right! These are variables, and they're used to remember information," Erin said, pointing to our answers. "You needed different types of things for the different parts of Maya's dress, right? So if this was a computer program, you'd be telling it what to add to the dress."

"Like what kind of button or collar or lace to pick," Maya said, her eyes wide.

"Exactly," Erin answered.

That made sense, but there was still a lot on the note that looked like gibberish to me.

"What does 'int' mean?" I asked, pointing to the top of the note.

"It's short for 'integers'—it's another word for whole numbers. Sometimes there are numbers with decimals in coding, but that wouldn't work here because you can't have half a button."

We chuckled.

"What about 'boolean'?" Sophia asked.

"A boolean's really simple: It's a type of data that only has two options: true or false," Erin explained.

"So, basically, whether or not the dress has sleeves," Sophia said.

"Uh-huh," Erin answered.

Maya chimed in. "And what about 'string'—what does that mean?"

"A string is simple, too: It's a word for a series of characters that can have letters, numbers, symbols, and punctuation marks in it."

"So 'petal' is a string, but something like 'Halverston#99' would be, too, if that made sense for the code?" I asked.

"Yup. And variables hold all kinds of data types, like integers, booleans, and strings, just like what you guys filled out here," Erin replied, pointing to our answers again.

I couldn't believe that what just looked like total nonsense made sense to me now.

"Erin, look how much we need you—please don't quit coding," I said, giving her my most pitiful, plaintive look.

Erin smiled sweetly. "You guys'll be fine without me. I've pretty much told you everything I know, anyway!"

I sensed that I wasn't going to be able to persuade her to stay in coding club—not as long as theater club was an option. But what if ...

I had the flyer for the hackathon tucked in with the coding notes, so I took it out of my pocket.

"Is that another note?" Erin asked, leaning over.

"No, it's a flyer I wanted to show you guys." I unfolded the paper.

Sophia took a peek at it. "Isn't that what we saw at the computer store?" I nodded.

"Calling all coders, don't miss the six-hour hackathon," Maya read out loud. "What's a hackathon?"

I smiled, trying not to let on my inner motive. "I looked

it up—it's a coding contest. You have to know some coding, but, Erin, with your help, I bet we could learn enough by then to win." I pointed at the prize money. "You could buy more cookbooks!"

"Um, I don't think she needs more books," Sophia said, with a sweeping motion of the boxes marked "books" in the kitchen and the living room.

"Or you could buy more shelves to put them on!" I suggested.

Everyone laughed, and Erin smiled sympathetically at me. "Sorry, Lucy," she said. "I can't. I really want to try theater, and I don't want to miss my chance."

We tried a few (million) more times to convince Erin to stay in coding club, but she was like a coding loop. She kept repeating, "While I can go to theater, I will go to theater," over and over again, which was disappointing, but also cracked us up. Eventually, we headed home.

That night, I couldn't stop thinking about the notes, especially now that I understood what they meant. I wondered if I'd receive more. But who could possibly be leaving them? I couldn't shake the idea that it was Alex. Still, that wasn't what was most on my mind—I was sad that Erin wasn't going to be in our coding group anymore. It wasn't like I'd known her that long, but I really liked hanging out with her, and I could tell Maya and Sophia did, too. Plus, it was obvious that she liked talking about coding. If only there was a way for her to do theater *and* coding club . . .

Chapter Eleven

The next day, I woke up with a plan.

The first thing I did was text Anjali. Then Maya and Sophia. And then I e-mailed Erin.

I went downstairs and cornered my brother, who was in the kitchen eating his cereal. It was just us at home—our parents were at a weekend-long conference for Mom's job.

"It's Sunday," Alex said, still wearing his pj's. "Don't bug me."

I sat on a stool next to him at the counter. "Alex, today is your big chance to be awesome."

"Too late." Alex grinned. "I've got all the awesome I need."

"Trust me, you need more," I said, rolling my eyes. "My friends are coming over, and we need your help." I gave him a stern look. "But real help. Not like hiding the toilet paper or putting oil in the soap dispenser. That's not helpful."

"But it's funny," Alex said with a smirk.

"Please," I said, acting serious. "We need your help with coding."

He thought about it for a second and said, "Okay."

"Really?" I asked. I had thought he'd need more convincing.

"Sure. I don't have work today," he answered. "And I don't mind helping out my little sis every now and then." He raised his eyebrows. "But I told you I can't help you with an app."

"No, it's not that," I said. "It's something different."

"'Kay, well, I'm around," he said, slurping down his cereal.

I eyed his smelly old pj's.

"Awesome, thanks! But can you put something . . . cleaner on before my friends get here?"

"Yes, your majesty," he said, fake-rolling his eyes, but then the day's second miracle happened—he went to his room to get changed.

Maya arrived first. Sophia got to the house a minute later.

"So . . . ," Maya started. "What's the deal?"

She was wearing purple shorts, a striped shirt, and cool socks with hearts on them. I felt underdressed in my ratty blue shorts and a sweater, but seeing as Sophia was in sports shorts, I let the feeling go. Now that I had gotten to know Maya, I knew she wasn't judging us.

"Is Erin coming over, too?" Sophia asked. "Your group text didn't include her."

"Not yet," I said, checking my phone. "Come upstairs! I want to show you guys something."

Sophia and Maya followed me up to my room. Sophia plopped down on the floor, and Maya and I sat on the bed. I grabbed my laptop, glanced at my screen, and crossed my fingers. *Please let Erin respond,* I thought to myself.

"I bet you want to know why I asked you to come over this morning," I said, sounding oddly formal.

Sophia and Maya looked at me, confused.

"Did you find out who's been leaving the notes?" Sophia asked.

"No, not yet." I glanced at my computer again.

Sophia looked at me worriedly. "What's going on, Lucy?"

"Yeah, what's going on?" Maya asked.

Finally, I couldn't hold it in anymore.

"Okay, so you guys know how Erin should be in coding club with us, right?" I said, trying to contain my excitement.

"Well, yeah, but she wants to do theater," Sophia said, reminding me of the obvious.

I looked down at my laptop and smiled mischievously.

"Wait, you aren't going to ruin that for her, are you, Lucy?" Maya sat up, concerned.

"Of course not!" I said. "I have an idea for how she can act *and* code, if she wants to." I turned my laptop toward them.

"I sent Erin three e-mails this morning." I showed them the first one:

```
if (you_want_to_act) {
    talk_to_Anjali ( );
}
```

"Love it," Maya said. "You used a conditional statement! But what does talking to Anjali have to do with anything?"

I smiled. I was proud of what I'd done. I only hoped it worked.

"Anjali isn't in theater club," I explained. "She's in film club. She told me that they're writing their own film, and they plan to submit it to student film festivals. Thing is, they need an actress who can sing." I let that sink in.

I could see a light in Sophia's eyes. She knew where I was heading.

"Here's the best part: Film club meets at the same time as coding club on Mondays, but they're using that time for production meetings. Anjali told me that the other night. They'll film on other days."

I paused to let that sink in, too.

"So . . . Erin could act for film club all week and code on Mondays!"

"Wow . . . that actually could work!" Sophia said.

Maya patted me on the back. "Good going, Lucy."

"Thanks! But there's one other thing—Anjali said Erin would have to audition," I added.

"You said she was good at voices. Is she good at singing, too?" Maya asked.

I was feeling pretty genius about it all. "I did a little research last night. Remember how Erin mentioned she was in the talent show at her old school?" I showed them the video of her performance. "Her mom uploaded it!" I grinned. "Sometimes it pays to have an embarrassing mom."

"Wow. Erin can dance, too," Sophia said. "I bet she'll get the role in the film, for sure."

"If she wants it, I think she'll be amazing," I said. "Now we just have to see if she followed the directions I sent."

Sophia was already looking at my second e-mail on the screen. "Oh, you're so funny. You created a loop!"

I'd written:

```
while (songs_left_to_sing) {
    write_code ( );
}
```

"I wanted to let her know she could sing *and* code," I said.

Maya smiled at me. "This is brilliant."

"But she hasn't responded yet," I said. "I thought that by now she'd have e-mailed back."

Sophia leaned in, "What was your third e-mail?"

I smiled. This was the most important one.

```
string friend_name_1 = "Maya";
string friend_name_2 = "Sophia";
string friend_name_3 = "Lucy";
string friend_name_4 = "_____";
```

"Wait." Sophia reread the e-mail on my computer. "Hang on, something isn't right."

"What?" I read the e-mail a few times. "I did the string

variable correctly, didn't I? The variable is the friend and the types are our names."

"That all looks right," Sophia said. "But, Lucy, you never pressed send!"

"Oh no!" I was feeling so clever, and then I forgot to do the last, most important, thing.

I hit send.

Then we stared at my inbox.

One minute passed. Then two. (Or at least it felt that way.)

Finally, an e-mail came back.

It read:

```
string friend_name_4 = "Erin";
```

"Oh my god, it worked!" I exclaimed.

"Awesome!" Sophia said, giving me a high five. Maya joined in, too.

We'd convinced Erin to stay in coding club *and* gotten her a gig for acting!

I texted her to tell her we were all hanging out at my place, and to come over. A few seconds later, I got a text back.

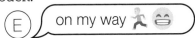

(E) on my way 🏃 😁

When Erin arrived, Alex answered the door and brought her upstairs.

I was grateful to see him wearing shorts and a clean T-shirt.

We all crowded around Erin. "I'm so happy you're here!" I gushed, giving her a big hug. She nearly dropped the tray of homemade cookies she'd brought.

"Middle-school girls are weird...," Alex muttered as he headed to the hall.

"No. Wait." I broke away from the others, and grabbed his arm. "Alex, stay."

"Oh right, you wanted my help. As long as no one starts hugging me," Alex said. "And I want a cookie," he added.

"Deal. So I've been getting these weird notes at school," I started telling him. I was willing to believe, at this point, that they weren't from him. We told him about each note.

"Wait a minute—you thought I was the one leaving you these notes all this time?" he said, genuinely surprised.

"Well, yeah..."

"And after wrongly accusing me, you want me to help you?"

I could tell he wasn't going to relent easily. "C'mon, Alex. We know what the coding stuff means now; we just want to figure out who wrote them."

Alex thought about it for a minute. I could tell he was intrigued. Finally, he suggested, "Why not use coding to catch the coder?"

I looked at the others, a smile forming. It actually wasn't a bad idea.

Chapter Twelve

*P*roblem was, our coding skills, even as a group, were pretty limited.

Alex started brainstorming ideas with us, but his girlfriend called, so he left soon after to talk to her on the phone. We hadn't gotten very far.

"Okay, so it's a good idea," Sophia said, biting into a cookie. "But how can we use coding to catch the note-leaver?"

"I used coding to talk to Erin," I said, considering the problem. "I'm sure we can come up with something."

Erin put her hair in a bun and tucked loose strands behind her ears. "Maybe we could create a program using what we know—input/output, conditionals, loops, and variables."

"We could try, but how would that help us find the note-leaver?" I said.

Erin thought about it. "Hmm ... I don't know."

"This is going to sound ridiculous," Maya said, "but so far, we haven't actually programmed anything on a computer. I mean, Lucy e-mailed Erin coding stuff, but that's different. How does actual coding even work? Don't we need some kind of special program?"

"I was wondering about that, too!" Sophia said.

"Can I see?" Erin pointed at my laptop. I handed it over to her and we all huddled around.

She went online and typed in a link. A big square with a black outline showed up on my computer screen.

"What's that?" Sophia asked.

"It's a website my dad and I use to write code," Erin answered. "We can type in the code here, and then copy and paste the link into a browser, and it'll play whatever program we coded."

Maya leaned in. "But it doesn't look like anything—it's just a box. How does it work?"

"It's a simple text editor," Erin said. "You can't use regular word processors for coding because they have formatting options, like changing fonts and stuff, that would get in the way of the code."

We all looked at her, confused. Erin started to type code, and the text and brackets appeared in a typewritten-looking font. "See? In a program like this, it's easier to see how your code lines up. Nothing gets in the way, so you can tell it exactly what you want it to do."

"So if we write code for a program here," I reasoned, trying to make sense of what she was saying, "we can make it, like, come alive?"

Erin laughed. "I'm not sure 'come alive' is the right way to put it, but yeah, if we code a game here, we could play it online. Or have someone else play it. We could even password protect it."

I thought about that for a second. "Okay, but even if we figure out how to code something, how are we going to get the coder to run it, if we don't know who that is?"

"Hmm...," Erin said, her fingers grazing the keyboard. It was so quiet, I swore I could hear the others thinking.

Alex stuck his head in. "So how's it going, *chicas*? Catch a coder yet?"

"Ugh, we don't know what to do," I told him, flopping back on my bed with a thud.

I think he could sense our frustration. "Maybe I can

help. What coding stuff have you guys learned so far?"

"We know about input/output and conditionals," I said.

"And variables," Maya added.

"And loops," Sophia chimed in.

Alex thought for a moment. "You could make a questions game," he suggested. "Ask things that only the person who left the notes might know."

That sounded good! "Whoever left the notes must have gone to the school playground recently," I said, feeling a bubble of excitement building inside. "They must have been there before me to set up the envelope under the bench."

"And whoever it was sent Lucy to the sports fields on Wednesday," Sophia said. "They might have even known I'd be there."

"And they knew what *variables* were missing from my dress," Maya added.

"And all the notes were on my locker, so it has to be someone who has access to the middle school," I said.

It felt like we were off to a good start.

"But even if we can code a game, how are we going to get people to play it? And who would we ask?" I wondered. "Alex, without you and Erin, we honestly don't have any other suspects."

Alex thought about that.

"Whoever is leaving the notes obviously knows a bit about coding. Where would there be kids who might know about variables, loops, and conditionals?"

"It can't be coding club, since we haven't learned any of that there yet," I said, racking my brain for who else in school might already know about coding.

"Wait a minute," Erin said, an idea forming. "Maybe there's someone else in coding club like me—someone who already knows coding, but didn't let it on at the first session."

"That *is* possible," Maya said, sitting up straighter. "And everyone saw how frustrated you were at coding club on Monday, Lucy, so someone from the club *could* be leaving you the notes."

"Good thinking!" Alex said. "Start with the kids in the club. I promise you that if you write this game, Mrs. Clark will be so impressed, she'll let everyone play it." He winked. "Believe me. She loves it when students show off their skills." He would know.

"But what if it's not someone in the club—" I started.

"Don't worry about that, Lu," Alex said. "With an 'if' statement, you can always have an 'else.'" He put it into code-speak. "*If* this game works, *then* you've solved the mystery; *else*, we think of something different to try."

We all laughed. We had a plan!

Maya, Sophia, Erin, and I made a list of ten questions that only the mystery coder would answer yes to, and Alex showed us how to use the coding concepts we'd learned to write the code.

We started with conditionals—if something happens, then the computer does something. Alex suggested that we outline our program on paper first in a format called pseudocode—he said it was a detailed description of what a computer program has to do, but told in normal language instead of programming language.

Erin had an idea. "If you were at the school playground," she suggested, "we could say 'Press the letter *Y*.' Then the key the user types could be stored as a variable. Right, Alex?"

"Exactly!" he said.

Alex helped us design an animation that would knock the player out of the program if they didn't answer yes, since we'd know that wasn't the person we were looking for. Maya drew five pictures of a rocket exploding, and Alex showed us how to use a loop to cycle through the pictures. We then used another loop to make our own GIF! This game was shaping up to be really cool.

When we finished the first question, the pseudocode looked like this:

```
question_1 = "Were you at the school playground
on Tuesday?";
show (question_1);
while (questions_left) {
  if (key_pressed_is_y) {
    show_next_question ( );
  }
  else {
    show_the_rocket_loop ( );
    end_the_program ( );
  }
}
```

We came up with more questions, and then typed them up. I couldn't believe that all those brackets and formatting that had seemed so strange to me were actually making sense! We figured out that if-then statements sometimes had "else" options where something "else" happened if the condition wasn't true. The rocket was part of an "else." So if the player pressed any key other than the letter *Y*, the rocket GIF we made appeared.

It took the five of us most of the day to code the game. By the time we finished, we were exhausted. I just hoped our plan was going to work the way we thought it would!

Chapter Thirteen

On Monday afternoon, it was finally time for our second coding club meeting. I couldn't believe only a week had passed since our first one—so much had happened.

On my way to Mrs. Clark's classroom, my phone vibrated. It was Anjali.

(A) Erin ROCKED her audition today!!! THANK YOU 🎉 🎉 👌

I grinned. The plan had worked!

I swung open the door to Mrs. Clark's classroom. Sophia, Maya, and Erin were already there, waiting for me at the back. We'd planned to meet early so we could talk to Mrs. Clark about the game before everyone in the club arrived. I went over to them and put my backpack down. We walked up to Mrs. Clark, who was sitting at her desk.

"Hi, Mrs. Clark," we said.

"Hi, girls," she said, glancing up from her computer. "Early for coding club?"

"Yup, and we have a surprise," I told her. Maya, Erin, Sophia, and I looked at one another excitedly.

"Oh really?" Mrs. Clark said, peering at us over her reading glasses. "What is it?"

"Well, we made a coding game, and we wanted to show it to you. Actually, we're hoping everyone in the club could play it," I explained. I hoped Alex was right and that she'd let us show it to the group.

"A coding game?" she said, taking her glasses off and setting them on her desk. "Wait a second—Lucy, didn't you complain that the club was moving too slowly last week?"

"Well . . . um," I stammered. "We figured out some things on our own." Maya, Erin, Sophia, and I exchanged conspiring looks.

"Did you now?" Mrs. Clark said. I could tell she was intrigued. "So tell me, how did you make this game?"

"We learned a few coding things this week," I said.

I didn't want to give away what we were doing until we caught the mystery coder. "So we used what we knew. Alex helped us a bit, but not a lot," I added.

She nodded. "Okay, can I take a look?"

We'd put the game on Alex's website and had password-protected it, so I gave Mrs. Clark the link and password, and she opened it up on her computer.

"I see . . . ," she said, smiling. "It's a question and answer game. Clever!"

She agreed to have the club try it out. I crossed my fingers that this was going to work.

By then, all the coding club kids had arrived.

"Okay, everyone!" Mrs. Clark said, clapping her hands to quiet everyone down. "We have something special today—a game!"

There was some cheering in the room. Mrs. Clark gave everyone the website and password and told them to give it a go. "And be honest when answering the questions, or the game won't work," she added.

My heart was racing as kids started playing the game. We could tell that some people were getting knocked out by rocket fire pretty quickly.

Bradley was the first to go. "Aw, man," he moaned as his

computer screen faded to black.

Sammy Cooper got pretty far, but he got knocked out, too.

When no one made it past seven questions, I figured the note-leaver wasn't anyone from coding club, after all.

"We need an *else* plan . . . ," I whispered to Erin.

As we started shuffling to our table at the back of the room, Mrs. Clark spoke up. "Can I try your game?" she said. "I see that you started with a conditional, used variables, and ended by looping a death-by-rocket animation. Good work."

It wasn't going to help us find the note-leaving culprit, but I didn't mind Mrs. Clark playing the game—I was proud for her to see how much we'd learned.

Mrs. Clark started the game on her computer. We stayed at the front of the room to see how she'd do.

She started by pressing *Y*. Yes, she'd been in the school playground on Monday.

Yes, she recently used a large yellow envelope.

Yes, she had a black scarf.

Yes, she knew what input/output meant.

Yes, she knew how to write a conditional.

Yes, she knew about loops.

Yes, she knew where Dress to Impress was located.

Yes, she had been there recently.

Yes, she had seen Maya's half-finished dress.

Yes, she understood string variables.

I couldn't believe what was happening. When Mrs. Clark finished the game, there was a looping popper GIF with exploding streamers that Alex and Erin had coded. The streamers kept falling until she pressed the escape key to end the game.

"Mrs. Clark?" I said, dumbfounded. "Was it you?"

She smiled at us.

"Yes, Lucy, I left the notes," she confessed. She turned to everyone in the club. "I actually gave notes to three of you, one from each table group, at the beginning of the week. I've been curious to see what happened."

"Wait, so we weren't the only ones solving coding mysteries all week?" Maya asked incredulously.

"Precisely," Mrs. Clark said.

We found out that Leila's group guessed from the first note who they were from, so Mrs. Clark swore them to secrecy. I had to give them credit for figuring it all out so fast and not telling anyone.

Bradley got the first note, but lost it, and when more

came, he couldn't figure out what they meant. He hadn't even shared them with his group.

"Girls," Mrs. Clark said, turning to us. "I'm so impressed with what you've done here. Why don't you explain the concepts you learned to everyone?"

We took turns telling the club what input/output, loops, conditionals, and variables were. It felt good to share what we'd learned in just one week.

"Thank you, girls. That was perfect. You can take your seats." We walked back to our group table, feeling proud of ourselves.

"Now we can start thinking about programs we want to create," Mrs. Clark said. "Nothing too complicated, and let's make it something that would be helpful around school," she quickly added.

I sighed. It looked like I wasn't going to be able to make the app for my uncle, after all. But that was okay—I knew it would probably be too complicated for me to do, at least now. I'd get there.

For the last five minutes of club time, Erin, Maya, Sophia, and I talked about ideas.

Maya proposed a clothes-swapping program, and Sophia wanted to make something to track sports scores.

But we all agreed that Erin's idea was the best.

We were going to make a program to help kids who were sick and missed school get their homework!

I grabbed a pen and a piece of paper from my backpack to take notes. Our program would match kids who were home sick with kids in their classes. It would have a way to keep track of homework and assignments. It would look for students who lived in similar neighborhoods to make delivery easy.

I wrote down our ideas, and added at the bottom:

This program will help everyone make new friends.

As I looked over the list, I noticed something odd happening to the words.

"What?!" I couldn't believe it. The list I had just written faded away, leaving a blank sheet of paper!

I thought for a moment. "Oh, Alex," I sighed. Disappearing ink, of course. He must have replaced my pens, and I hadn't noticed. He'd been so helpful, but now he was back to being himself. I shouldn't have expected any less from him.

I sighed even harder when I remembered that I'd used

the same pen to write notes in English class on index cards. I must not have noticed because I was turning the cards so fast. Ugh!

I reached into my bag to grab a pencil. As I leaned down, the hackathon flyer in my jacket pocket from a few days ago caught my eye. It was only a month away. We'd already learned so much in just one week, at this rate, I was sure we'd know enough coding by then to sign up. I just had to convince the others. I was about to talk to them about it when Mrs. Clark came over to our group.

"I'm so impressed with what you did here today, girls. Coding is about teamwork and problem-solving, which is exactly what you did this past week. I'd like to make the four of you a permanent group for coding club, if that's okay."

Sophia, Erin, Maya, and I all looked at one another and nodded. We *already* were a permanent group. And I had a feeling that our catch-the-coder game was just the beginning.

Acknowledgments

There were a lot of amazing coders involved in this book. I want to thank the staff at Girls Who Code. Special thanks go to the awesome coding girls in my neighborhood: Annie Chang and Sophie Courtney.

My gratitude extends to Aria Lin, Matt Cohen, Laura Sebastian, and Mai Robinson—I couldn't have done this without you as my very own "permanent" group.

With heartfelt appreciation to my agent, Deborah Warren.

If you want to learn more about how to code, don't miss *Girls Who Code: Learn to Code and Change the World,* available August 2017!